Happy Birthday,

Roger,

Jack Gerard

A Painter of Our Time

Permanent Red

The Foot of Clive

Corker's Freedom

The Success and Failure of Picasso *

A Fortunate Man *

Art and Revolution *

The Moment of Cubism and Other Essays

The Look of Things: Selected Essays and Articles

Ways of Seeing

Another Way of Telling *

A Seventh Man

Pig Earth *

'G' *

About Looking *

Our Faces, My Heart, Brief as Photos *

The Sense of Sight *

* Available from Pantheon

ONCE IN EUROPA

JOHN BERGER

ONCE
IN
EUROPA

PANTHEON BOOKS
NEW YORK

"Boris Is Buying Horses" and "The Accordion Player"
previously appeared in *Granta* no. 9 (1983) and no. 18
(1986) respectively, and "Play Me Something" in
The Threepenny Review no. 20 (winter 1985).

Library of Congress Cataloging-in-Publication Data
Berger, John.
Once in Europa.
1. Love stories, English. I. Title.
PR6052.E56405   1987   823'.914   86-25287
ISBN 0-394-53992-3
ISBN 0-394-75164-7 (pbk.)

Book design by Susan Mitchell
Manufactured in the United States of America
First American Edition

ACKNOWLEDGMENT

I would like to acknowledge with affection and
gratitude the support I received from the
Transnational Institute, Washington, D.C.,
during the long years I spent writing this book.

CONTENTS

Weathered as gate posts
by departures
and the white ghosts
of the gone,
wrapped in tarpaulins,
we talk of passion.
Our passion's the saline
in which hides are hung
to make from a hinge of skin
the leather of love.

This is the second volume of the trilogy *Into Their Labours.** *Pig Earth*, the first volume, was a book of stories set against the traditional life of a mountain village. Certain details apart, this village could exist in a number of countries across the continents of the world.

Once in Europa, the second volume, is a collection of love stories set against the disappearance or "modernisation" of such village life.

The third volume will tell the story of peasants who leave their villages to settle permanently in a metropolis.

* *"Others have laboured and ye are entered into their labours."* John 4:38.

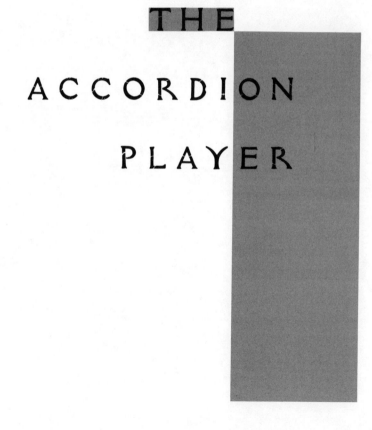

THE
ACCORDION
PLAYER

Will you play at my wedding? Philippe the cheese-maker asked him. Philippe was thirty-four. People had been saying he would never get married.

When is it?

Saturday next.

Why didn't you ask me before?

I didn't dare. Will you?

Where does the bride come from?

Yvonne comes from the Jura. Drop into the Republican Lyre tonight and she'll be there—her parents have come and some friends from Besançon.

The same evening the accordionist, a man in his fifties, found himself sitting in the café, drinking champagne offered by the bride's father, next to a plump woman who laughed a lot and wore dangling earrings. The accordionist had been looking hard at the young bride and he was sure she was pregnant.

You will play for us? Philippe asked, filling up the glasses.

Yes, I'll play for you and the Yvonne, he said.

On the floor at his feet lay a dog, its coat turned grey with age. From time to time he caressed its head.

What's your dog's name? asked the woman with earrings.

Mick, he said, he's a clown without a circus.

He's old to be a clown.

Fifteen Mick is, fifteen.

You have a farm?

At the top of the village—a place we call Lapraz.

Is it a big farm?

Depends who's asking the question, he answered with a little laugh.

Delphine is asking you the question.

He wondered if she was often drunk.

Well, is it a big farm? she asked again.

One winter the mayor asked my father: Have you got a lot of snow up at Lapraz? And do you know what Father replied? Less than you, Mr. Mayor, he said, because I own less land!

That's beautiful! Delphine said, knocking over a glass as she put a hand on his shoulder. No fool, your father.

Have you come for the wedding? he asked her.

I've come to dress the bride!

Dress her?

It was me who made the wedding dress and there are always finishing touches to make on the Great Day!

Are you a dress-maker? he asked.

No! No! I work in a factory . . . I just pin things up for myself and friends.

That must save you money, he said.

It does, but I do it because it amuses me, like you play the accordion, they tell me . . .

You like music?

She disentangled her arms and held them wide apart as though she were measuring a metre and a half of cloth. With music, she sighed, you can say everything! Do you play regularly?

Every Saturday night in the café, weddings excepted.

This café?

No, the one at home.

Don't you live here?

Lapraz is three kilometres away.

Are you married? she asked, looking him straight in the eye. Her own eyes were grey-green like the jacket she was wearing.

Unmarried, Delphine, he replied. I play at other men's weddings.

I lost my husband four years ago, she said.

He must have been young.

In a car accident . . .

So quick! He pronounced the two words with such finality that she was silenced. She fingered the stem of her glass, then lifted it to her lips and emptied it.

You like playing the accordion, Félix?

I know where music comes from, he said.

THAT IT WAS going to be a bad year had been evident to Félix from the moment in the spring when the snow thawed. All around the village there were pastures which looked as though they had been ploughed up the previous autumn and they hadn't been. In the orchards the fruit trees were growing out of mud instead of grass. The earth every-where was like an animal whose fur was falling out. All this was due to the invasion of the moles. Some maintained that the moles had multiplied so catastrophically because the foxes had died or been shot the year before. A fox eats thirty or forty moles a day. The foxes had died because of the rabies which had been brought to our region from the distant Carpathians.

He was standing motionless in the garden in front of his house. Across his body he was holding a spade. He had been like that for ten minutes. He was looking at the earth just ahead of his boots. Not a grain of soil stirred. Towards the mountain, a buzzard was circling, otherwise nothing in sight was moving. The leaves of the cabbages and cauliflowers in the garden were wilted and yellow. With one hand he could have lifted any one of these plants off the earth, as you lift a candlestick off a table. All their roots had been severed.

When he saw the soil stir, he raised his spade and struck,

grunting as the spade entered the earth. He kicked the soil away. There were the disclosed tunnels and the dead culprit mole.

One less! he said, grinning.

Albertine, Félix's mother, was watching her forty-year-old son through the kitchen window when he killed the mole with the spade. She shouted to him to come in because the meal was on the table.

With today's sun, she said whilst they were eating, the potatoes shouldn't be dirty.

They shouldn't be, he replied.

The pup under the table looked up, hoping for a bone or some cheese-rind. He was large and black with blond marks shaped like almonds over each eye which made him look comic.

Ah, Mick! said Félix, our Mick's a clown without a circus, isn't he?

If you like, said Albertine, I'll make potato fritters tonight.

With cabbage salad! He took off his cap and smeared his sleeve across his hot forehead. Why not?

Years before, when Albertine had been strong enough to work in the fields, they used to lift the potatoes together. Whilst working they would recite all the ways in which potatoes could be eaten: potatoes in their jackets, potatoes with cheese in the oven, potato salad, potatoes with pork fat, mashed potatoes with milk, potatoes cooked without water in the black iron saucepan, potatoes with leeks in the soup—and, best of all, potato fritters with cabbage salad.

The potatoes, unearthed that same morning, had dried well in the sun on the topsoil of the field. As Félix gathered them by hand into buckets, he sorted them. The small ones for the animals and poultry, the large ones for the table. Sometimes he moved forward stooping, sometimes he knelt between the rows and went forward on his knees, like a penitent. Mick, panting in the heat, lay on the ground and each time Félix moved forward, he accompanied him. When the buckets were full the man emptied the potatoes into sacks along the side of the field. The sacks were of strong white plastic and had contained fertiliser. When they were full, they looked liked praying drunks in white shirts.

Suddenly the dog became alert, his head down, nose in the broken earth. Breathing out heavily, he started to scrabble with his front paws and to scatter the soil behind him.

Fetch him! Mick, fetch him! Félix sat back on his heels to watch the young dog. He was happy to be diverted and to rest his back, which ached. The dog continued to dig excitedly.

You want him, Mick, don't you?

At last the dog deposited a mole on the earth.

You have him, don't let him go!

The dog tossed the mole into the air. For an instant the little animal in its grey fur coat, measuring fifteen centimetres in length and weighing a hundred and fifty grammes, with paws like hands, with very weak eyesight and acute hearing, renowned for his testicles and the exceptional amount of seminal fluid they produced, for an instant the little animal was hapless and alone in the sky.

Quick, Mick!

Fallen back onto the soil, the mole, no longer capable of flight, began to squeal.

Have him!

The dog ate the mole.

Alone in the house, Albertine asked herself for the hundredth time the same question: when she was gone, what would Félix do? Men, she considered, were strong-backed, reckless and weak, each man combining these essential qualities in his own way. Félix needed a woman who would

not take advantage of his weakness. If the woman were am-
bitious or greedy, she would exploit him and use his strong
back and his recklessness to ride him where she wanted. Yet
now he was forty and the woman had not been found.

There had been Yvette. Yvette would have cuckolded him,
just as she was now cuckolding the poor Robert whom she
married. There had been Suzanne. One Sunday morning, just
before Félix did his military service, she had seen him caressing Suzanne on the floor beneath the blackboard in the schoolroom—the same schoolroom where he had learnt as a boy!
She had crept away from the window without disturbing
them, but she repeatedly reminded her son, when she wrote
to him in the army, that school teachers can't sit on milking
stools. Suzanne had left the village and married a shopkeeper.

Was it going to be worse for her son to be alone than to
have married the wrong woman? This question made Albertine
feel as helpless as she had sometimes felt as a child.

In the evening Félix emptied the sacks full of potatoes into
a wooden stall in the cellar under the house. Potatoes just
lifted from the earth give off a strange warmth and in the
darkness of the cellar they glow like children's shoulders
after a day in the sun. He looked at the heap critically: there
were going to be far less than last year.

Did you finish? asked Albertine when he entered the
kitchen.

Four more rows to do, Maman.

I've just made the coffee . . . Get under the table! You're
not firm enough with that pup, Félix.

He caught five moles this afternoon.

Are you going out tonight?

Yes, there's a meeting of the Dairy Committee.

Félix drank the coffee from the bowl his mother handed
him and began reading the Communist Party paper for
peasants and agricultural workers.

Do you know where the biggest bell in the world is, Maman?

Not round the neck of one of our cows!

It's called the Tsar Kolokol, it weighs 196 tons and was cast in Moscow in 1735.

That's a bell I'll never hear, she said.

When he went into the stable to start milking, she took out his suit from the wardrobe which her husband had made one winter when they were first married, and brushed the trousers with the same energy as she had once groomed their mare. Then, having laid the suit on the high double bed beneath her husband's portrait, she did something she had never done before in her life. She took off her boots and lay, fully-clothed, on top of the bed.

She heard Félix come back into the kitchen, she listened to him washing by the sink. She heard him taking off his trousers and washing between his legs. When he had finished, he came into the bedroom.

Where are you? he asked.

I'm taking a rest, she said from the bed.

What's the matter?

A rest, my son.

Are you ill, Maman?

I feel better now.

She watched him dress. He stepped into the trousers with the creases which she had ironed. He put on the white cotton shirt buttoned at the cuffs, which showed off his handsome shoulders. He slipped into the jacket—he was putting on weight, no question about that. Nevertheless he was still handsome. He ought to be able to find a wife.

Why don't you go to a dentist? she asked. He glanced at her, puzzled.

He could arrange your teeth.

I haven't a toothache.

He could make you more handsome.

He could also make us poorer!

Let me see you in your cap.

He put it on.

You're even more handsome than your father was, she said.

When Félix returned to the farm that night, he was surprised to see a car, its lights on, parked outside the house. He entered hurriedly. The doctor from the next village was in the kitchen washing his hands in the sink. The door to the Middle Room was shut.

If there's no improvement by the morning, your mother will have to go to the hospital, the doctor said.

Félix looked through the kitchen window at the mountain opposite, which, in the moonlight, was the colour of a grey mole, but he could not see around what had happened.

What happened? he asked.

She telephoned your neighbours.

She won't want to go to the hospital.

I have no choice, said the doctor.

You're right, said Félix suddenly furious, it is her choice which counts!

You can't look after her properly here.

She has lived here for fifty years.

If you're not careful, she may die here.

The doctor wore glasses and this was the first thing you noticed about him. He looked at everything as if it were a page to read. He had come straight to the village from medical school full of idealism. Now, after ten years, he was disillusioned. Mountain people did not listen to reason, he complained, mountain people drank too much, mountain people went on repeating what they thought they had once heard as children, mountain people never recognised a rational process, mountain people behaved as if they thought life itself was mad.

Have a drink before you go, Doctor.

Does your mother have a supplementary insurance?

Which do you prefer, pears or plums?

Neither, thank you.

A little gentian? Gentian cures all, Doctor.

No alcohol, thank you.

How much do I owe you?

Twenty thousand, said the doctor, adjusting his glasses.

Félix took out his purse. She has worked every day of the year for fifty years, he thought, and tonight this shortsighted quack asks for twenty thousand. He extracted two folded bank notes and placed them on the table.

The doctor left and Félix went into the Middle Room. She was so thin that, under the eiderdown, her body was invisible. It was as if her head, decapitated, had been placed on the pillow.

An expression of irritation, like that on a dog's muzzle when it sniffs alcohol, ruffled her face whilst her eyes remained closed. When the spasm was over, her face resumed its calm, but was older. She was ageing hour by hour.

Noticing the dog lying on the floor at the foot of the bed, Félix hesitated. She would have insisted on the dog being put out.

Not a sound, Mick!

He climbed onto the bed beside his mother so that he would be reassured by her breathing throughout the night. She stirred and, turning on the pillow, asked for some water. When he gave her the glass, she could not raise her head. He had to hold her head up with his hand, and her head seemed to weigh nothing, to be no heavier than a lettuce.

They both lay there, awake and without saying a word.

You'll get the rest of the potatoes in tomorrow? she eventually asked.

Yes.

Next spring there'll be fewer moles, she said. There won't be enough for them all to eat to survive the winter.

They breed quickly, Maman.

In the long run such troubles correct themselves, she insisted, if not by next year, by the year after. Yet you, you, my son, you will always remember the Year of the Thousand Moles.

No, Maman, you're going to get better.

The next day whilst he was cutting wood on the circular saw, Félix stopped every hour to go into the house and reassure himself. Each time, lying on the large bed, her arms straight by her side, she opened her eyes and smiled at him.

Everything was ready and prepared, she knew, in the second drawer of the wardrobe. Her black dress with the mother of pearl buttons, the black kerchief with blue gentian flowers printed on it, the dark grey stockings, and the shoes with laces which would be easier to put on than boots. How many times had Marie-Louise promised to come and dress her if it was she, Albertine, who was the first to go?

That night after Félix had come to lie down beside her, she said: It's years, my boy, since you played your accordion.

I don't even know where it is.

It's in the grenier, she said, you used to play so well, I don't know why you stopped.

It was when I came out of the army.

You let it drop.

Father was dead, there was too much to do.

He glanced at the portrait hanging above the bed. His father had a thick moustache, tiny comic eyes and a strong neck. He used to tap his neck, as if it were a barrel, when he was thirsty.

Would you play me something? Albertine asked.

On the accordion?

Yes.

After all this time I won't get a breath out of it.

Try.

He shrugged his shoulders, took the electric torch off its hook on the wall, and went out. When he came back he extracted the accordion from its case, arranged one strap round his shoulder and, slipping his wrist under the other, started to pump. It worked.

What tune do you want?

"Dans tes Montagnes."

The two voices of the accordion, tender and full-blown, filled the room. All her attention was fixed on him. His body was rolling slowly to the music. He has never been able to make up his mind, she reflected, it's as if he doesn't realise this is his only life. I ought to know since it was I who gave birth to him. And then, carried away by the music, she saw their cows in the alpage and Félix learning to walk.

When Félix stopped playing, Albertine was asleep.

Neighbours came to visit the house, bringing with them pears, walnut wine, an apple tart. Albertine repeatedly declared she had no need of anything except water. She stopped eating. She would take whatever messages they wanted, she would pray with them for what they thought they needed, she would bless them, but she would accept no pity and no competition. She was the next to leave.

To the old man, Anselme, she whispered: Try to find him a wife.

It's not like our time, he said, shaking his head. Nobody wants to marry a peasant today.

I'm glad you say that, she said.

I'm not saying Félix couldn't get married, answered Anselme pedantically. I'm simply saying women of his generation married men from the towns.

It's the idea of his being left alone.

I've been alone for twenty years! It's twenty years now since Claire died and I can recommend it. He chuckled.

Abruptly Albertine lowered her head to indicate that it was his duty to kiss her whilst she prayed. Obediently Anselme kissed the crown of her head.

She was now so weak and thin that Félix was frightened of smothering her when he slept. One night he woke up from a dream. He listened for her breathing. Her breath was as weak as an intermittent breeze in grass waiting to be scythed. Through the lace curtains he could see the plum trees his father had grafted. The light of the moon going down in the west was reflected in the mirror behind the wash bowl.

In the dream he had again been a conscript in the army. He was walking along a road, playing an accordion. Behind him was a man carrying a sheep. It was he, Félix, who had stolen the sheep, or, rather, a young woman had given the sheep to him on condition that . . . and he had taken the sheep knowing full well . . .

The dream became vaguer and vaguer as, awake, he saw something else. He saw Death approaching the farm. Or, rather, he saw Death's lamp, bobbing up and down, as Death strode leisurely past the edge of the forest where the beech trees in October were the colour of flames, down the slope of the big pasture which drained badly at the bottom, under the linden tree full of wasps in August, over the ruts of the old road to St. Denis, between the cherry trees against which, every July, she asked him to lean the long ladder, past the water trough where the source never froze, beside the dung-heap where he threw the afterbirths, through the stable into the kitchen. When Death entered the Middle Room—where the smoked sausages were hanging from the ceiling above the bed—he saw that what he had taken to be a lamp was in fact a white feather of hoarfrost. The feather floated down onto the bed.

Abruptly Albertine sat up and said: Fetch me my dress, it is time to go!

The day after the funeral, when Félix delivered his milk to the dairy, he surprised everyone there by his cheerfulness.

Have you ever worked as a butcher? he asked Philippe, the cheese-maker. No? Well, you'd better take a correspondence course—with diagrams! Next year there's going to be no hay, no cows, no milk, no bonus for cream, no penalty for dirt . . . We're all going to be in the mole-skin business! That's what we are going to be doing . . .

The absence of the mourned is as precise as their presence once was. Albertine's absence was thin with arthritic hands and long grey hair gathered up in a chignon. The eyes of her absence needed glasses for reading. During her lifetime many cows had stepped on her feet. Each of her toes had been stepped on by a cow on a different occasion, and the growth of its nail consequently deformed. The toenails of her absence were the yellow of horn and irregularly shaped. The legs of her absence were as soft to touch as a young woman's.

Every evening he ate the soup he had prepared, he sliced the bread, he read the Communist Party paper for peasants and agricultural workers, and he lit a cigarette. He performed these acts whilst hugging her absence. As the night drew on and the cows in the stable lay down on their bedding of straw and beech leaves, the warmth of his own body penetrated her absence so that it became his own pain.

On All Souls' Day he bought some chrysanthemums, white ones the colour of goose feathers, and placed the pot of flowers, not by the tombstone in the churchyard, but on the marble-top commode in the Middle Room beside the large empty bed.

A week later the snow came. The children ran screaming out of school, impatient to build snowmen and igloos. When Félix delivered his milk to the dairy, he repeated the remark that Albertine had made every year when the first snow fell:

Let it snow a lot tonight, let the snow get so high our hens can peck the stars!

Through the kitchen window he stared at the white mountain. Mick was licking a plate on the floor.

The winter's long, it would be better if we could sleep.

The dog looked up.

Who do you think is going to win the elections? The same gang as before, eh?

The dog started wagging his tail.

Do you know what you like and what they manufacture in Béthune? Do you know, Mick?

Félix strode across the kitchen towards the massive dresser. To take something off its top shelf it was necessary to stand on a chair. Its doors, with their square panes of glass and their bevelled window frames, were big enough for a cow to go through.

So you don't know, Mick, what they manufacture in Béthune? From the bottom shelf he picked up a packet of sugar.

Sugar, Mick, sugar is what they manufacture in Béthune! Brusquely he threw two lumps towards the dog. Three more. Six. Then he emptied the whole packet. Fifty lumps of sugar fell onto the floorboards in a cloud of dust.

Sugar in Béthune! Milk here! He shouted the words so violently the dog hid under the table.

One day in January he noticed that the floorboards, instead of being bread-coloured, were now grey like slates. He put the dog out, he stoked up the stove with wood, he took off his boots and trousers and began scrubbing on his knees. He had left it too long, the dirt was engrained. He ground his teeth, he refilled and refilled the bucket with water from the giant saucepan on the stove. The planks slowly changed colour.

The more he scrubbed, the more he saw the countless washings the floor had undergone as but a single instant in an eternity of dust and neglect. He straightened his back and looked up at the dresser. On the top shelf was their best china, decorated with sprays and garlands of flowers: violets, forget-me-nots, honeysuckle. The way the flowers were painted around the rims of the plates, in the hearts of the dishes, on the flanks of the bowls, made him think of ears, mouths, eyes, breasts.

He put on his trousers and boots, laid down sheets of newspaper and stepping from one sheet to another reached the door. Outside it was snowing grey snow. He teetered like a drunk into the stable and there, his forehead resting on one of his cow's haunches, he vomited till there was nothing left in his stomach.

■ ■ ■

A few days later he beat the cow Myrtille. Myrtille had the bad habit of butting the cow next to her. If he showed Myrtille a stick, this was usually enough to deter her. She glowered at him with her insolently tranquil eyes, and he brandished the stick in the air and said: The bow of the violin, eh! Is that enough or do you want some music!

On the evening in question he forgot the stick and Myrtille knocked him off his stool whilst he was preparing her neighbour's teats before plugging the milking machine onto her. Seizing a rake, he beat Myrtille across the haunches with the handle. She put her head down and he beat her harder. He was beating her now because she had reduced him to beating her. She lay down on the floor and he beat her out of the fury of his knowledge that he could not stop beating her.

In the name of God! he spat out the words as if they were his own broken teeth. Nothing! Nobody!

The shock of each blow was transmitted to his shoulders. Then the handle of the rake broke.

It seemed to him that the animal never forgave him.

Towards the end of March the giant bedspread of packed snow began to slide down the roof of the house a few centimetres each day. After a while, a border of packed snow overhanging the roof would crack and fall to the ground in a thousand pieces. In the cellar, despite the darkness and the thickness of the walls, the potatoes were putting out pink-violet shoots. The force of these shoots is so strong that they can pierce canvas or denim as if they were thin air.

A week earlier the doctor had asked him: Are you still vomiting? Do you want some more pills?

Félix had replied: No, Doctor . . . what I need is an extra pair of hands. Can you give me a prescription for that? Preferably a woman's hands, but I'll accept a man's or even a boy's.

Thus he confirmed one of the doctor's favourite dinner-table dissertations: namely, that the dearth of women in the valley—the best men having left with the women following them—was pushing the idiots who remained towards homosexuality and even bestiality.

In twenty-hour hours a well-fed cow shits a wheelbarrow of dung. The winter had lasted a hundred and fifty days and Félix had seventeen cows. He recalled the time, before they bought a tractor, when all the winter's dung had to be forked into a tip cart, hauled by the horse and unloaded in heaps, to be spread out again with a fork over the fields. Now he had a mechanical shovel and a spreader. And now he was alone.

Albertine had been right: there were fewer mole hills. Many moles must have died, the strongest eating the weakest. In the morning when he started up the tractor it was freezing. By midday on the hillside with the spreader, he was sweating. This year he refused to take off his sheepskin jacket. If he caught cold and fell ill, there would be nobody else to milk the cows. His solitude had strange ramifications. His trousers caked with cowshit went on stinking until he himself put them in the washing machine. Sometimes the solitude of the house smelt acrid like cowshit.

Every evening, sitting at the table beneath the clock that was always half an hour fast so that he would not deliver the milk too late at the dairy, he decided what to do the following day. Shit till Sunday, Mick, or shall we do the wood?

During the winter it had been a question of killing time. Now time was resurrected. He forgot obvious things. He fed the chickens and forgot the eggs. He hadn't collected eggs from the hen house since he was seven when his father went away for the second time. The first time his father went away was for his military service, the second time was when he went to Paris to earn the money to re-cover the roof of the house with tiles; it took him four winters to earn enough.

How often had he heard his father tell the story of his time in the army. Soldier Berthier! Why did you not obey the order given to you? Replied his father: One of you tells me to do this, another of you tells me to do that, another of you tells me to do something else, so what am I to do? Just tell me clearly what you want and I'll do it! Soldier Berthier! Clean out this room! One of you tells me to do this, another one tells me to do that . . . To every order, his father replied in the same way. Soldier Berthier, one month's detention! He was put in a cell. Prisoner Berthier, are you a good shot? You tell me clearly what you want, and I'll do it. The Company needs a good marksman, Berthier! He was taken out and given a rifle and five bullets. He scored five bull's-eyes. For the rest of his military service he had no duties and no fatigues. All he had to do was go occasionally and shoot in the regimental competitions on the rifle range. When his father finished the story, he always added: On this earth, Felo, you need to be clever.

In April he planted his potatoes. It was as hot that year in April as it usually is in June. Walking slowly along the drill, he dropped a potato between his legs every twenty centimetres. Sometimes the potato fell badly and he was forced to bend down to place it properly.

There are some who know where to go, Mick, and some that have to be put in their place!

Each time he chose with his eyes the exact place between

the clods where he hoped the potato would fall. If he did not do this, it fell badly.

The last potato planted, he climbed towards the house. It was almost noon. Suddenly he stopped in his steps. High above the roof a swarm of bees was flying away from the sun towards the north.

Rushing into the kitchen, he came out with a large saucepan and a metal soup ladle. He ran through the orchard rattling the ladle in the saucepan. Mick was barking at his heels. When he was ahead of the swarm, he drummed harder than ever, and held the saucepan so that it glinted in the sun and flashed like a mirror. The swarm, subject to a single will, made straight for the nearest plum tree and settled on one of its branches.

Now he could take his time. He found an empty hive and rubbed its inside with plum leaves. He strolled over to the outhouse to fetch a saw. He sawed off the branch on which the bees were settled and carried it over to the hive. There he tapped the branch smartly with a plank and the swarm fell off like a wig.

If the Queen is there, they'll stay. If not, they'll leave tomorrow.

It was then that he heard his mother's voice calling him by name. The sound the bees were making gave birth to her voice, and at the same time muffled it. The voice went on repeating his name as if the solitude of his days were now in the name itself.

Each season loads up men as if they were wheelbarrows and then wheels them forward to do its tasks. Félix ploughed the field for the alfalfa. One day, when he was twelve, in the field he was now ploughing, his father had said to him:

Do you want to come hunting with me?

They climbed, both of them, to the forest below Peniel.

We'll wait here, Felo, and do nothing. Shut your mouth and keep your eyes skinned.

His father cut some branches from a beech tree and arranged them like a light screen in front of them. The beech leaves, just unfurled, were as fresh-looking as lettuces. They waited behind the screen for what seemed to Félix an eternity. The bones in his body began to ache one by one because he didn't dare move a limb. His father sat there as patient as if he were listening to music, his gun between his knees. From behind a spruce twenty metres away, a wild boar appeared, hesitated, and then walked, like a confident habitué, across their vision. The father fired. The boar keeled over and lay down as if inexplicably overcome by sleep.

Do you know what's important in this life, Felo?

No, Papa.

Good health. And what does good health give you? It gives you a steady hand.

The father prodded the animal with his boot.

Guard him! he said and disappeared down the path to the village. Félix sat on his heels beside the dead boar, whose small eyes were open. When his father returned with a sledge across his back, he was panting hard but grinning. Together they tied the carcass—it weighed a good hundred and fifty kilos—onto the light sledge. Then they started the difficult journey down.

Father Berthier put himself between the two wooden arms in the position of a two-legged horse. Like this he could pull when the runners of the sledge met an obstacle or when the slope wasn't steep enough, and like this, if they were running too fast over the mud or the new slippery grass, he could brake by digging in his heels and lifting up the front of the sledge so that its weight leant backwards and the back of the sledge was forced into the ground. Félix followed, holding onto a rope to brake the speed, but in fact being pulled along ever faster. One false step on his father's part and the charging boar and sledge would knock him onto his face and ride over him.

His last run home, Felo!

Not so fast, Papa!

The boy had his father's gun across his back.

When they were down on the road which passes the café, they stopped to give their legs a rest.

It's the knees, isn't it, which feel it?

My legs aren't tired, lied the boy.

There's a man for you!

Along the grass bank by the side of the road the sledge slid gently and easily. The boy let go of the rope and put the gun under his arm, carrying it like a hunter.

They met Louis, who could argue a politician under the table.

The month of May, the season for hunting? asked Louis.

It's no gazelle! said his father.

I'd hide him quick if I were you, said Louis. How many shots?

One shot, only one shot. Felo here is going to be a hunter. His hand's as steady as a rock.

And Félix, although he knew why his father, cunning as ever, had invented this story, was filled with pride.

When they got home and the boar had been hidden in the cellar, his father said: It's time you learnt to use a gun, I'll find you one. What do you say to that?

I'd rather have an accordion, replied Félix.

An accordion! Ah! you want to seduce the girls, eh?

One night, a few months later, Félix was in bed and he

heard his father come into the kitchen, shouting in the sing-song voice which meant he had been drinking. There were some other men with him who were laughing. Then there was a silence, and, suddenly, the strains of an accordion being clumsily played. I got it for Felo, he heard his father shout, got it off Valentine. She was glad to be rid of it, now Emile's dead, what could she do with an accordion? Poor Emile! said another voice. She never liked him playing, said a third man, she'd walk out of the room as soon as Emile picked the thing up. How's that? She was jealous was our Valentine and Emile encouraged her to be so. He liked to make her jealous! Do you know what he named his accordion? What did he call it? He called his accordion Caroline! Come and sit on my knees, Caroline, he'd say, come and have a cuddle! All you men are the same! Félix heard his mother protest. Come and sit on my knees, Albertine! his father roared, come here and I'll give you a squeeze! He pressed on the bass buttons and the instrument lowed like a bull. You'll wake up Félix, you will! his mother said.

It was a diatonic accordion with twelve bass keys for the left hand, made by F. Dedents in the 1920s. The keys had pearly heads, its sides were blue decorated with yellow flowers, and the reeds were made of metal and leather. He learnt to play it seated, resting the right-hand keyboard on his left thigh and opening the accordion like a cascade falling towards the floor to the left of the chair. A cascade of sound.

Late in the month of May, the grass grows before your eyes. One day it is like a carpet, the next it is halfway up your knees. Get it scythed, Albertine would say, or it'll be tickling the cunt.

The cows in Félix's stable could smell the new grass. They followed with their insolently patient eyes the two swallows who were building a nest on the cross beam above the horse's stall, empty since the purchase of the tractor. They stared at the squares of sunlight on the north wall which had been in shadow all winter long. They became restless. They lowed for Félix before it was milking time. They wouldn't eat their croquettes quietly whilst being milked. When they licked each other with their large tongues, they did so with a kind of frenzy, as if the salt they were tasting had to be a substitute for all the green grass outside.

They want to be out, don't they? They don't need a calendar to tell them, and they don't give a fuck what year it is. Tomorrow we'll put 'em out, tomorrow when the grass is dry.

Late the following morning Félix undid each cow's chain and opened the large door of the stable.

Myrtille turned towards the sudden light and felt her neck free. Then she tottered, like a convalescent, to the door. Once outside, she raised her head, bellowed and trotted in the direction of the green grass she could see in the meadow. With each step she found her strength again.

Hold her back, Mick!

The dog bounded after the cow and barked at her forelegs so that she stopped, her neck stretched out taut and straight, her ears up like a second pair of horns, and her imperturbable eyes staring through the sunshine at the meadow. Immobile, her muzzle, her neck, her haunches and her tail in one straight line, she was like the first statue ever made of a cow. The other cows were pushing through the stable door three at a time.

Calm, for Christ's sake! There's enough for you all. Get back, Princesse!

They trundled their way down the slope towards Myrtille. Mick saw the whole herd charging at him. His mouth open without a bark, without a whine, he slunk to the side of the

road as they thundered past and triumphantly swept Myrtille
into the field. As soon as they felt their feet in the grass, their
stampede ended. Some threw their hind legs up into the air.
One pair locked their horns and shoved against each other
with all their weight. Some turned slowly in circles, listening.
The streams from the mountains above the village, white with
froth because so much ice had melted, were babbling like
madmen. The cuckoo was singing. Entire fields were suddenly changing their colour from green to butter-yellow, because the dandelions, shut at night, were opening their petals.

Princesse mounted Mireille—when a cow is in heat, she
often plays the bull.

Get her off her!

Mireille, with Princesse on her back, stood gazing at the
mountains. The sunshine penetrated to the very marrow of
their bones. When the dog approached, Princesse slid gently
off Mireille's back, and the wind from the northwest, from
beyond the mountains, ruffled the hair between both their
horns.

Félix arranged the wire across the opening to the field,
switched on the current, and, plucking a stalk of hemlock,
held it against the live wire. After a second his hand shot up
like a startled bird. He returned slowly to the house, stopping
twice to look back at the happiness of the cows.

He phoned the Inseminator to ask him to pass by for
Princesse and gave him the code number of her previous
insemination.

In making hay there's always a wager. The quicker the hay
is in, the better it is. Yet the hay must be dry, otherwise it
ferments. At the worst, tradition had it, damp hay could
eventually set a house on fire. If you don't take any risks you'll

never get your hay in early. At the best, you'll be left with hay like straw. So, impatient, you bet on the sun lasting and the storm holding off. It's not us making hay, repeated Albertine every year, it's sun that makes the hay.

This lottery made haymaking something of a fête. Each time they won they had cheated the sky. Sometimes they won by minutes, the first drops of rain falling as the horse pulled into the barn the last cart of the hay cut two days before. The hurry, the women and children in the fields, the sweat washed away with spring water, the thirst quenched with coffee and cider, being able to jump from a height of fifteen feet in the barn to land deliciously unharmed in the hay, the hay which he knew how to untangle and comb, the barn as tall as a church slowly filling up until, on top of the hay, his head was touching the roof, the supper in the crowded kitchen afterwards, this had all made haymaking a fête during the first half of his life.

Today he was alone, alone to decide the risks, to cut the hay, to ted it, to turn it, to windrow it, to load it, to transport it, to unload it, to pack it, to level it, to quench his thrist, to prepare his own supper. With the new machines he did not have to work harder than in the first half of his life; the difference now was that he was finally alone.

He had cut half the grass in what his father always called Grandma's Field. It was on the slope above the linden tree. The hay had been turned but still needed a good hour's sunshine. It was hot and heavy, the weather for horseflies. He studied the sky as if it were a clock to tell him how many hours away the storm might be. Then he bent down to pick up another handful of hay, assessing its dryness with his fingers. There were four trailer-loads to bring in. He decided to give it half an hour before windrowing. He switched off the tractor engine and walked over to the edge of the field where there was a strip of shade from a little ash grove. There he lay down and pulled the cap over his eyes. He tried to remember the cold of winter but couldn't. He thought he heard thunder in the distance and jumped to his feet.

Get it in now, Felo.

He walked back towards the tractor along the edge of the unmown half of the field where the grass was green and the flowers still coloured. The compagnon rouge, pink like lipstick. The tiny vetch scattered like stars of creamy milk. The bellflower, mauve, head bowed. The deep blue mountain cornflower, which cures conjunctivitis, its calyx crisscrossed with black lace like the stockings of dancers. As he noticed them he picked them. Herb bennett, yellow like a scarf. Crepide fausse blathaire, vigorous cropped blond. Fragrant orchid, red like a pig's penis. He began to pick quickly and indiscriminately in order to make a bouquet, the first since he left school.

Get it in now, Felo.

He drove the tractor back to the house, unhooked the tedder and attached the windrower. The flowers he stuck into a jam jar which he filled with water from the kitchen tap.

The storm broke as he was bringing the last load in.

Saved by the skin of our teeth, Mick!

In the barn he was stripped to the waist. His stomach and back, so rarely exposed to the air, were as pale as a baby's. When you looked at him you thought of a father as seen by his child. Perhaps this was because his own flesh looked both manly and childish.

When he had unloaded the trailer it was time to begin the milking. He walked out into the rain. He could feel it cooling his blood. It ran down his back into the inside of his trousers. Then he put on his vest and his tartan shirt, threw the blue cap onto his wet hair, switched on the motor for the milking machine and went into the stable. He left the door open, for there was little light inside and his eyes still smarted from the hay dust.

The milking finished, he entered the kitchen. He had closed the shutters as Albertine had always insisted upon doing in the summer to keep the room cool. Light from the sunset filtered between their slats. On the window sill was the bunch of flowers he had picked. On seeing them he stopped in mid-stride. He stared at them as if they were a ghost. In the stable a cow pissed; in the kitchen the stillness and silence were total.

He pulled a chair from under the table, he sat down and he wept. As he wept his head slowly fell forward until his forehead touched the oilcloth. Odd how sounds of distress are recognised by animals. The dog approached the man's back and, getting up on its hind legs, rested its front paws on his shoulder blades.

He wept for all that would no longer happen. He wept for his mother making potato fritters. He wept for her pruning the roses in the garden. He wept for his father shouting. He wept for the bobsled he had as a boy. He wept for the triangle of hair between the legs of Suzanne the schoolmistress. He wept for the smell of a woman ironing sheets. He wept for jam bubbling in a saucepan on the stove. He wept for never being able to leave the farm for a single day. He wept for the farm where there were no children. He wept for the sound of rain on the rhubarb leaves and his father roaring: Listen to that! That's what you miss when you go away to work for months, and when you come back in the spring and hear that sound you say, Thank God in Heaven I'm home! He wept for the hay, still to be brought in. He wept for the forty-two years that had gone by, and he wept for himself.

In July the evenings seem endless. When Félix, his boots full of hayseed and his face tear-stained, took his two churns of milk to the dairy, he could see for miles across the valley towards the mountains. Most of the fields were mown. Because he was alone, he would always be the last to finish his hay. The heat gone, the shaved ground lay there in a kind of trance waiting for hares or lovers. He drove faster than usual, cutting the corners. His tyres screeched as he braked. There were already five other cars there. He kicked open the door as if he wanted to break it down. The cheesemaker and the other peasants who had delivered their milk looked at him quizzically. He poured his churn into the tub on the scales without glancing at the reading. And when he emptied the tub into the vat he did so with a ferocity that wiped the smile off the others' faces. The milk splashed the wooden ceiling. His second churn he emptied the same way.

Everything all right at home, Félix?

Nothing, nobody to complain about.

Have a glass of rouge? Albert, the old man, lifted a bottle off a shelf above the sink. Félix declined and left.

For God's sake! muttered one of them shaking his head.

In a year or two, said Albert, he'll start drinking. Men aren't made to live alone. Women are stronger, they merge with the weather, I don't know how.

Find him a wife!

He'll never marry.

Why do you say that?

Too late.

It's never too late.

To set up house with a woman, yes, it's too late.

He'd make a good husband.

It's a question of trust, insisted Albert.

Whose trust?

After forty a man doesn't trust a woman enough.

Depends on the woman.

Any woman.

In God's name!

Suppose he finds an old maid—he'll say to himself: there must be something the matter with her, nobody else wanted her. Suppose he finds a woman who's divorced—he'll say: she did wrong by one man, she may do the same to me. Suppose he finds a widow—he'll say: she's been a wife once, it's my farm she's after! With age we all become a little meaner.

And what if he finds a young woman who's unmarried?

Ah! my poor Hervé, said Albert, you say that because you're still young yourself. If Félix finds a virgin—

Virgin!

No matter! Suppose he finds a young woman, he'll say to himself—and who knows? he might be right—he'll say to himself: in a year or so she's going to cuckold me as sure as day follows night . . .

The men laughed, Albert handed out a glass of wine, and they watched, idly, the white liquid heating in the copper vat, the white liquid that only starts flowing after a birth. Outside the sky was darkening faintly and the first stars were like sleep in its eyes.

Félix, already back in the kitchen, was reading the Communist Party paper for peasants and agricultural workers.

Do you know where the biggest bell in the world is, Maman?

Not round the neck of one of our cows!

It's called the Tsar Kolokol, it weighs 196 tons and was cast in Moscow in 1735.

That's a bell I'll never hear, she said.

Suddenly he got up from the table and walked across the bare floorboards into the Middle Room. From under the large bed he pulled out the accordion case and came back with the instrument in his arms. There was no longer enough light to read by, yet he did not switch on the light. Instead, he opened the door to the stable and entered its darkness. He felt with his foot for the milking stool that he kept by the water tap and he sat down on it. Myrtille eyed him, another cow mooed. And in the stable, a yard from the gutter full of the cows' greenish shit, he began to play. The air, hot with the heat of the animals who had spent the day in the sun, smelt strongly of garlic, for wild garlic grows in the field by the old road to St. Denis where they had been grazing. The instrument breathed in this air and its two voices smelt of it. He played a gavotte in quadruple time. Gavotte, which comes from gavot, meaning mountain dweller, meaning goitre, meaning throat, meaning cry.

Most of the cows were bedded down. At first they turned their heads to where the music was coming from and the ears of those who were nearest went up, querying, yet very soon they discovered that the music represented nothing more than itself, and their ears relaxed and they put their heads again on their own flanks or on a neighbour's shoulder. One of the swallows flew around like a bat, less easily reassured than the cows. As he played, Félix looked towards the small window beside the door. The stars were no longer like sleep in the corner of its eye, but like rivets. His head was rigid, only his body moved with the music.

Now he was playing "Le Jeune Marchois," a plaintive wedding march he'd learnt in the army from a friend who came from Limoges. Two fingers of his left hand, their nails broken, their knuckles engrained with dirt, the chapped tip of one cracked by the cold of winters, played a staccato beat which was as high and raucous as the cry of a corncrake. His right hand, raised level with his shoulder, was playing the melody which rose and fell like a chain of hills, a chain of gentle hills, of hillocks, of young breasts. His head was now nodding to the tune, his boot on the cobblestones tapping to

the beat. The wedding procession approached and the undulating hills gave way to a hedgerow behind which appeared, disappeared and reappeared women with glistening
stoles thrown over their shoulders. The calls of the corncrake
too were transformed. No longer the cries of a bird, they were
the whistle of air emitted from a leather bag punctured by
the point of a knife. His two fingers hit the keys like rivet
chargers. The procession had risen in the east by his right
shoulder, now it was midday and was before his eyes. Each
woman had removed her stole, and the white linen undulating
in the wind caressed the bare shoulders of the woman behind
her. The women could see the procession of men approaching.
The whistles of air were gasps of breath. Appearing and dis-
appearing behind the branches of the hedgerow, the women
were undoing their hair. Yet already they were passing to
the west. The gasps of breath became again the cry of a
corncrake, more and more distant, disturbed, fleeting. The
road behind the hedge was deserted. A mist covered the hills.

A cow shat when he ceased playing. A pungent smell of
wild garlic was wafted towards him. He remembered the waltz
of "Rosalie de Bon Matin." He played it as loud as he could.

It was due to Louis, who can still argue a politician under
the table, that Félix began to play regularly every week in the
café at Lapraz. One evening the following winter Louis went
to try to sell Félix a ticket for a lottery which was being
organised to raise money to pay for the transport of the village
children to the nearest swimming pool. Everyone born in the
mountains should learn how to swim! was the motto of the
campaign.

There I was, explained Louis afterwards in the café,
climbing up through the orchard to Felo's house. It was al-

ready dark and I was glad I had a pocket lamp. At the top
of the hill I thought I heard music. It must be the radio, I
told myself. My hearing's not as good as it used to be. From
the big pear tree beside the yard a white owl flew up. There's
not many come up this way at night, I said. The music was
clearer now, and it was an accordion. No radio sounds like
that. The crafty boy, he's got company, I said. Nearer the
house, I couldn't believe my ears. The music was coming
from the stable! There was a light in the window and the
music was coming from the stable! Perhaps he's dancing with
the gypsies, perhaps he likes to dance with gypsies and is
frightened to let them into the house, thieving good-for-
nothings that they are. Who would have believed Felo would
dance with gypsies if he wasn't his father's son? I peered
through the filthy little window and inside I could make out
the dancing figures. No use knocking here, Lulu, I said. So I
tried the door. It was locked. To hell with the lottery ticket, I
simply wanted to see what was going on. All the doors were
locked and he was with the gypsies in the stable. Then I had
an idea. Ten to one, Félix didn't lock the barn door above the
house. Up the ramp in five seconds and I was right, it was
open. By each trap he'd prepared the hay to fork down to each
cow in the morning. Not everyone does that, he's farsighted,
Félix. The music was coming up through the floorboards
louder and wilder than ever—a mazurka. I lifted up one of the
traps and, lying on my stomach on the little pile of hay, I
peered through. There was the cow bedded down, and there
was Félix seated on a stool, beneath the one dim electric light
bulb, an accordion between his arms. For the rest I couldn't
believe my eyes. Lulu, you're seeing things, I told myself.
Félix was alone! Not another soul in the stable, playing to
the fucking cows! He can play though, Félix can. You should
get him to bring his music down here sometime.

ON THE NIGHT of Philippe's wedding, when the sky was already getting light from the dawn, long after Philippe had taken Yvonne to bed, and the parents and the parents-in-law had gone home, a few of us, including the dressmaker with dangling earrings who liked laughing and who worked in a factory that produced wooden handles for house painters' brushes, a few of us were still dancing and Félix sat playing on his usual chair, his cap on the back of his bald head, his heavy working-boots tapping the floor as he played. We might have stopped dancing before, yet one tune had led to the next, and Félix had fitted them together like one pipe into another till the chimney was so high it was lost in the sky. A chimney of tunes, and the women's feet so tired they had taken off their shoes to dance barefoot.

Music demands obedience. It even demands obedience of the imagination when a melody comes to mind. You can think of nothing else. It's a kind of tyrant. In exchange it offers its own freedom. All bodies can boast about themselves with music. The old can dance as well as the young. Time is forgotten. And that night, from behind the silence of the last stars, we thought we heard the affirmation of a Yes.

"La Belle Jacqueline" once more! the dressmaker shouted at Félix. I love music! With music you can say everything!

You can't talk to a lawyer with music, Félix replied.

Perhaps they are right, those who pretend there are harps in heaven. Maybe flutes and violins too. But I'm sure there are no accordians, just as I'm sure there's no green cowshit that smells of wild garlic. The accordion was made for life on this earth, the left hand marking the bass and the heart-beats, the arms and shoulders labouring to make breath, and the right hand fingering for hopes!

Finally we stopped dancing.

Come on, Caroline, come on, Félix muttered as he made his way alone to the door. It's time to go.

BORIS

IS

BUYING

HORSES

Sometimes to refute a single sentence it is necessary to tell a life story.

In our village, as in many villages in the world at that time, there was a souvenir shop. The shop was in a converted farmhouse which had been built four or five generations earlier, on the road up to the mountain. You could buy there skiers in bottles, mountain flowers under glass, plates decorated with gentians, miniature cowbells, plastic spinning wheels, carved spoons, chamois leather, sheepskins, clockwork marmots, goat horns, cassettes, maps of Europe, knives with wooden handles, gloves, T-shirts, films, key rings, sunglasses, imitation butter-churns, my books.

The woman who owned the shop served in it. She was by then in her early forties. Blond, smiling but with pleading eyes, pleading for God-knows-what, she was buxom, with small feet and slender ankles. The young in the village nick-named her the Goose—for reasons that are not part of this story. Her real name was Marie-Jeanne. Earlier, before Marie-Jeanne and her husband came to the village, the house belonged to Boris. It was from him that they inherited it.

Now I come to the sentence that I want to refute.

Boris died, said Marc, leaning one Sunday morning against the wall that twists like the last letter of the alphabet through our hamlet, Boris died like one of his own sheep, neglected and starving. What he did to his cattle finally happened to him: he died like one of his own animals.

Boris was the third of four brothers. The eldest was killed in the War, the second by an avalanche, and the youngest emigrated. Even as a child Boris was distinguished by his brute strength. The other children at school feared him a little and at the same time teased him. They had spotted his weakness. To challenge most boys you bet that they couldn't lift a sack of seventy kilos. Boris could lift seventy kilos with ease. To challenge Boris you bet him that he couldn't make a whistle out of a branch of an ash tree.

During the summer, after the cuckoos had fallen silent, all the boys had ash whistles, some even had flutes with eight holes. Having found and cut down the little branch of wood, straight and of the right diameter, you put it in your mouth to moisten it with your tongue, then tapped on it, all round, briskly but not too hard with the wooden handle of your pocket knife. This tapping separated the bark from the wood so that you could pull the white wood out, like an arm from a sleeve. Finally you carved the mouthpiece and reinserted it into the bark. The whole process took a quarter of an hour.

Boris put the little branch into his mouth as if he were going to devour the tree of life itself. And his difficulty was that he had invariably struck too hard with his knife handle, so that he had damaged the bark. His whole body went tense. He would try again. He would cut another branch and when it came to tapping it, either he would hit too hard, or, with the concentrated effort of holding himself back, his arm wouldn't move at all.

Come on, Boris, play us some music! they teased him.

When he was fully grown, his hands were unusually big and his blue eyes were set in sockets which looked as though they were meant for eyes as large as those of a calf. It was as if, at the moment of his conception, every one of his cells had been instructed to grow large; but his spine, femur, tibia, fibula had played truant. As a result, he was of average height but his features and extremities were like those of a giant.

One morning in the alpage, years ago, I woke up to find all the pastures white. One cannot really talk of the first snow of the year at an altitude of 1,600 metres, because often it snows every month, but this was the first snow which was not going to disappear until the following year, and it was falling in large flakes.

Towards midday there was a knock on the door. I opened it. Beyond, almost indistinguishable from the snow, were thirty sheep, silent, snow on their necks. In the doorway stood Boris.

He came in and went over to the stove to thaw out. It was one of those tall stoves for wood, standing free in the centre of the room like a post of warmth. The jacket over his gigantic shoulders was white as a mountain.

For a quarter of an hour he stood there silent, drinking from the glass of gnôle, holding his huge hands over the stove. The damp patch on the floorboards around him was growing larger.

At last he spoke in his rasping voice. His voice, whatever the words, spoke of a kind of neglect. Its hinges were off, its windows broken, and yet, there was a defiance in it, as if, like a prospector living in a broken-down shack, it knew where there was gold.

In the night, he said, I saw it was snowing. And I knew my sheep were up by the peak. The less there is to eat, the higher they climb. I drove up here before it was light and I set out. It was crazy to climb by myself. Yet who would come with me? I couldn't see the path for the snow. If I'd lost my foothold, there was nothing, nothing at all, to stop me till I reached the churchyard below. For five hours since daybreak I have been playing against death.

His eyes in their deep sockets interrogated me to check whether I had understood what he was saying. Not his words, but what lay behind them. Boris liked to remain mysterious. He believed that the unsaid favoured him. And yet, despite himself, he dreamed of being understood.

Standing there with the puddle of melted snow at his feet, he was not in the least like the good shepherd who had just risked his life for his flock. St. John the Baptist, who crowned the Lamb with flowers, was the very opposite of Boris. Boris neglected his sheep. Each year he sheared them too late and they suffered from the heat. Each summer he omitted to pare their hooves and they went lame. They looked like a flock of beggars in grey wool, Boris's sheep. If he had risked his life that day on the mountain, it wasn't for their sake, but for the sake of their market price.

His parents had been poor, and from the age of twenty Boris boasted of the money he was going to make one day. He was going to make *big* money—according to the instructions received at his conception and inscribed in every cell of his body.

At market he bought cattle that nobody else would buy, and he bought at the end of the day, offering a price which twelve hours earlier would have appeared derisory. I see him, taciturn beside the big-boned animals, pinching their flesh with one of his immense thumbs, dressed in khaki and wearing an American army cap.

He believed that time would bring him nothing, and that his cunning must bring him everything. When he was selling he never named his price. You can't insult me, he said, just tell me what you want to offer. Then he waited, his blue, deep-set eyes already on the brink of the derision with which he was going to greet the price named.

He is looking at me now, with the same expression. I told you once, he says, that I had enough poems in my head to fill a book, do you remember? Now you are writing the story of my life. You can do that because it's finished. When I was still alive, what did you do? Once you brought me a packet of cigarettes whilst I was grazing the sheep above the factory.

I say nothing. I go on writing.

The uncle of all cattle dealers once told me: A ram like Boris is best eaten as meat.

Boris's plan was simple: to buy thin and sell fat. What he sometimes underestimated was the work and time necessary between the two. He willed the thin cattle to become fat, but their flesh, unlike his own, was not always obedient to his will. And their bodies, at the moment of conception, had not received the same instructions.

He grazed his sheep on every scrap of common land and often on land which wasn't common. In the winter he was obliged to buy extra hay, and he promised to pay for it with lambs in the spring. He never paid. Yet he survived. And his herd grew bigger: in his heyday he owned a hundred and fifty sheep. He drove a Land Rover which he had recuperated from a ravine. He had a shepherd whom he had recuperated from an alcoholics' clinic. Nobody trusted Boris, nobody resisted him.

The story of his advancement spread. So too did the stories of his negligence—his unpaid debts, his sheep eating off land which belonged to other people. They were considered a scourge, Boris's sheep, as if they were a troop of wild boar. And often, like the Devil's own, his flock left and arrived by night.

In the Republican Lyre, the café opposite the church, there was sometimes something of the Devil about Boris too. He stood at the bar—he never sat down—surrounded by the young from several villages: the young who foresaw initiatives beyond the comprehension of their cautious yet wily parents, the young who dreamed of leisure and foreign women.

You should go to Canada, Boris was saying, that's where the future belongs. Here, as soon as you do something of your own, you're mistrusted. Canada is big, and when you have something big, you have something generous!

He paid for his round of drinks with a fifty-thousand note, which he placed on the counter with his wooden-handled knife on top of it, so that it wouldn't blow away.

Here, he continued, nothing is ever forgiven! Not this side of death. And, as for the other side, they leave it to the curé. Have you ever seen anyone laughing for pleasure here?

And at that moment, as though he, the Devil, had ordered it, the door of the café opened and a couple came in, the woman roaring with laughter. They were strangers, both of them. The man wore a weekend suit and pointed shoes, and the woman, who, like her companion, was about thirty, had blond hair and wore a fur coat. One of the young men looked out through the window and saw their car parked opposite. It had Lyons licence plates. Boris stared at them. The man said something and the woman laughed again. Her laughter was like a promise. Of what? you may ask. Of something big, of the unknown, of a kind of Canada.

Do you know them?

Boris shook his head.

Shortly afterwards he pocketed his knife, proffered the fifty-thousand note, insisted upon paying for the two coffees the couple from Lyons were drinking, and left, without so much as another glance in their or anybody else's direction.

When the strangers got up to pay, the patronne simply said: It's already been settled.

Who by?

By the man who left five minutes ago.

The one in khaki? asked the blond. The patronne nodded.

We are looking for a house to rent, furnished if possible, said the man. Do you happen to know of any in the village?

For a week or a month?

No, for the whole year round.

You want to settle here? asked one of the youths, incredulous.

My husband has a job in A——, the blond explained. He's a driving instructor.

■ ■ ■

The couple found a house. And one Tuesday morning, just before Easter, Boris drew up in his Land Rover and hammered on the door. It was opened by the blond, still wearing her dressing gown.

I've a present for you both, he said.

My husband, unfortunately, has just gone to work.

I know. I watched him leave. Wait!

He opened the back of the Land Rover and returned with a lamb in his arms.

This is the present.

Is it asleep?

No, slaughtered.

The blond threw her head back and laughed. What should we do with a slaughtered lamb? she sighed, wiping her mouth with her sleeve.

Roast it!

It still has its wool on. We don't know how to do such things and Gérard hates the sight of blood.

I'll prepare it for you.

It was you who bought us the coffee, wasn't it?

Boris shrugged his shoulders. He was holding the lamb by its hind legs, its muzzle a few inches from the ground. The blond was wearing mules of artificial leopard skin.

Come in then, she said.

All this was observed by the neighbours.

The hind legs of the lamb were tied together and he hung it like a jacket on the back of the kitchen door. When he arrived, the blond had been drinking a bowl of coffee which was still on the table. In the kitchen there was the smell of coffee, of soap powder and of her. She had the smell of a buxom, plump body without a trace of the smell of work.

Work has the smell of vinegar. He put out a hand to touch her hips as she passed between the table and the stove. Once again she laughed, this time quietly. Later he was to recall this first morning that he found himself in her kitchen, as if it were something he had swallowed, as if his tongue had never forgotten the taste of her mouth when she first bent down to kiss him.

Every time he visited her, he brought her a present; the lamb was only the first. Once he came with his tractor and trailer and on the trailer was a sideboard. He never disguised his visits. He made them in full daylight before the eyes of his neighbours, who noticed that each time, after about half an hour, the blond closed the shutters of the bedroom window.

And if one day her husband should come back unexpectedly? asked one of the neighbours.

God forbid! Boris would be capable of picking him up and throwing him over the roof.

Yet he must have his suspicions?

Who?

The husband.

It's clear you've never lived in a big town.

Why do you say that?

The husband knows. If you'd lived in a big town, you'd know that the husband knows.

Then why doesn't he put his foot down? He can't be that cowardly.

One day the husband will come back, at a time agreed upon with his wife, and Boris will still be there, and the husband will say: What will you have as an aperitif, a pastis?

And he'll put poison in it?

No, black pepper! To excite him further.

■ ■ ■

Boris had been married at the age of twenty-five. His wife
left him after one month. They were later divorced. His wife,
who was not from the valley, never accused him of anything.
She simply said, quietly, that she couldn't live with him. And
once she added: perhaps another woman could.

The blond gave Boris the nickname of Little Humpback.

My back is as straight as yours.

I didn't say it wasn't.

Then why—

It's what I like to call you.

Little Humpback, she said one day, do you ski?

When could I have learned?

You buy the skis and I'll teach you.

I'm too old to start, he said.

You're a champion in bed, you could be a champion on
the ski slopes!

He pulled her towards him and covered her face and
mouth with his huge hand.

This too he was to remember later when he thought about
their two lives and the differences between them.

One day he arrived at the house carrying a washing machine
on his shoulders. Another day he came with a wall-hanging
as large as a rug, on which were depicted, in bright velvet
colours, two horses on a mountainside.

At that time Boris owned two horses. He'd bought them on
the spur of the moment because he liked the look of them and
he'd beaten down their price. In the spring I had to deliver a
third horse to him. It was early morning and the snow had
melted the week before. He was asleep in his bed and I woke

him. Above his bed was a Madonna and a photograph of the
blond. We took a bale of hay and went out to the field. There
I let the horse go. After a long winter confined to the stable,
she leapt and galloped between the trees. Boris was staring at
her with his huge hands open and his eyes fixed. Ah Freedom!
he said. He said it in neither a whisper nor a shout. He simply
pronounced it as if it were the name of the horse.

The blond hung the tapestry on the wall in the bedroom. One
Sunday afternoon, when Gérard was lying on the bed watching television, he nodded at the tapestry where the horses'
manes were combed by the wind as if by a hairdresser and the
horses' coats gleamed like polished shoes and the snow be-
tween the pine trees was as white as a wedding dress, and he
said:
  It's the only one of his presents I could do without.
  I like horses, she said.
  Horses! He made a whinnying noise.
  Your trouble is that horses scare you!
  Horses! The only thing to be said about a picture—and
that's a picture even if it is made out of cotton—
  Velvet!
  —same thing, the only thing to be said about that picture
there—is that in a picture horses don't shit.
  In your mind everything's shit, she said.
  Have you talked to him about the house yet? Gérard asked.
  I'll talk to him when I choose.
  Calling him Little Humpback's not bad!
  She turned off the TV.
  I call him, Gérard, whatever I love to call him. He's my
business.

■ ■ ■

How difficult it is to prevent certain stories becoming a simple moral demonstration! As if there were never any hesitations, as if life didn't wrap itself like a rag round the sharpest blade!

One midday, the following June, Boris arrived at the blond's house, covered in sweat. His face, with his hawk-nose and his cheekbones like pebbles, looked as if he had just plunged it into a water trough. He entered the kitchen and kissed her as he usually did, but this time without a word. Then he went to the sink and put his head under the tap. She offered him a towel which he refused. The water from his hair was running down his neck to the inside of the shirt. She asked him whether he wanted to eat; he nodded. He followed her with his eyes wherever she went, not sentimentally like a dog, nor suspiciously, but as though from a great distance.

Are you ill? she asked him abruptly as she put his plate on the table.

I have never been ill.

Then what is the matter?

By way of reply he pulled her towards him and thrust his head, still wet, against her breast. The pain she felt was not in her chest but in her spine. Yet she did not struggle and she placed her plump white hand on the hard head. For how long did she stand there in front of his chair? For how long was his face fitted into her breast like a gun into its case lined with velvet? On the night when Boris died alone, stretched out on the floor with his three black dogs, it seemed to him that his face had been fitted into her breast ever since he first set eyes on her.

Afterwards he did not want to eat what was on his plate.

Come on, Humpback, take your boots off and we'll go to bed.

He shook his head.

What's the matter with you? You sit there, you say nothing, you eat nothing, you do nothing, you're good for nothing!

He got to his feet and walked towards the door. For the first time she noticed he was limping.

What's the matter with your foot?

He did not reply.

For Christ's sake, have you hurt your foot?

It's broken.

How?

I overturned the tractor on the slope above the house. I was flung off and the fender crushed my foot.

Did you call the doctor?

I came here.

Where's the jeep?

Can't drive, can't move the ankle.

She started to untie the boots. She began with the unhurt foot. He said nothing. The second boot was a different matter. His whole body went rigid when she began to unlace it. His sock was drenched in blood and the foot was too swollen for her to remove the boot.

She bit her lip and tried to open the boot further.

You walked here! she exclaimed.

He nodded.

Seated on the kitchen floor at his feet, her hands limp by her side, she began to sob.

His foot had eleven fractures. The doctor refused to believe that he had walked the four kilometres from his farm to the blond's. He said it was categorically impossible. The blond had driven Boris down to the clinic, and, according to the doctor, she had been at Boris's house all morning but for some reason didn't want to admit it. This is why, according to the doctor, the two of them had invented the implausible story of his walking four kilometres. The doctor, however, was wrong.

Of all the many times that Boris visited her, this was the only one which she never once mentioned to Gérard. And when, later, she heard the news of Boris's death, she abruptly and surprisingly asked whether he was wearing boots when they found him.

No, was the reply, he was barefoot.

Boris, when young, had inherited three houses, but all of them, by the standards of the towns, were in a pitiable condition. In the house with the largest barn he himself lived. There was electricity but no water. The house was below the road and the passerby could look down its chimney. It was in this house that the three black dogs howled all night when he died.

The second house, the one he always referred to as the Mother's house, was the best situated of the three and he had long-term plans for selling it to a Parisian—when the day and the Parisian arrived.

In the third house, which was no more than a cabin at the foot of the mountain, Edmond, the shepherd, slept when he could. Edmond was a thin man with the eyes of a hermit. His experience had led him to believe that nearly all those who walked on two legs belonged to a species named Misunderstanding. He received from Boris no regular salary but occasional presents and his keep.

One spring evening, Boris went up to the house under the mountain, taking with him a cheese and a smoked side of bacon.

You're not often at home now! was how Edmond greeted him.

Why do you say that?

I have eyes. I notice when the Land Rover passes.

And you know where I go?

Edmond deemed the question unworthy of a reply, he simply fixed his unavailing eyes on Boris.

I'd like to marry her, said Boris.

But you can't.

She would be willing.

Are you sure?

Boris answered by smashing his right fist into his left palm. Edmond said nothing.

How many lambs? asked Boris.

Thirty-three. She is from the city isn't she?

Her father is a butcher in Lyons.

Why hasn't she any children?

Not every ram has balls, you should know that. She'll have a child of mine.

How long have you been going with her?

Eighteen months.

Edmond raised his eyebrows. City women are not the same, he said, and I ought to know. I've seen enough. They're not built the same way. They don't have the same shit and they don't have the same blood. They don't smell the same either. They don't smell of stables and chicken mash, they smell of something else. And that something else is dangerous. They have perfect eyelashes, they have unscratched legs without varicose veins, they have shoes with soles as thin as pancakes, they have hands white and smooth as peeled potatoes and when you smell their smell, it fills you with a godforsaken longing. You want to breathe them to their dregs, you want to squeeze them like lemons until there is not a drop or a pip left. And shall I tell you what they smell of? Their smell is the smell of money. They calculate everything for money. They are not built like our mothers, these women.

You can leave my mother out of it.

Be careful, said Edmond, your blond will strip you of

everything. Then she'll throw you aside like a plucked chicken.

With a slow blow to the face Boris knocked the shepherd over. He lay spread-eagled on the ground.

Nothing stirred. The dog licked Edmond's forehead.

Only somebody who has seen a battlefield can imagine the full indifference of the stars above the shepherd, spread-eagled on the ground. It is in the face of this indifference that we seek love.

Tomorrow I will buy her a shawl, whispered Boris, and without a glance behind him, took the road back to the village.

Next morning the police came to warn him that his sheep were a public danger, for they were encumbering the highway. Edmond the shepherd had disappeared and he was not seen again until after Boris's death.

The month of August was the month of Boris's triumph. Or is glory a better term? For he was too happy, too self-absorbed, to see himself as a victor who had triumphed over others. It had become clear to him that the instructions inscribed at the moment of his conception had involved more than the size of his bones, the thickness of his skull or the power of his will. He was destined, at the age of forty, to be recognized.

The hay had been brought in, his barn was full, his sheep were grazing high in the mountains—without a shepherd but God would preserve them—and every evening he sat on the terrace of the Republican Lyre overlooking the village square, with the blond in a summer dress, her shoulders bare, her feet in high-heeled silver sandals, and until nightfall the pair of them were the colour-television picture of the village.

Offer drinks to every table, he said, leaning back in his chair, and if they ask what's happened, tell them that Boris is buying horses!

Humpback, not every night, you can't afford it!

Every night! My balls are swollen.

He placed one of his immense hands on the bosom of her red polka-dot dress.

It's true about the horses, he said, I'm going to breed horses —for you! Breed riding horses that we'll sell to the idiots who come for weekends.

What should I do with horses? she asked, I can't ride.

If you have a child of mine—

Yes, Humpback.

I'll teach the child to ride, he said. A child of ours will have your looks and my pride.

The last word he had never before uttered concerning himself.

If we have a child, she whispered, the house where we live now is too small. We'd need at least another room.

And how many months have we got to sort out the question of a house? asked Boris with his cattle dealer's canniness.

I don't know, Humpback, perhaps eight.

A bottle of champagne, Boris shouted, pour out glasses for everybody.

Are you still buying horses? asked Marc, who, with his pipe and blue overalls, is the sceptic of the Republican Lyre, the perennial instructor about the idiocy of the world.

That's none of your business, retorted Boris. I'm buying you a drink.

I'll be tipsy, said the blond.

I'll get you some nuts.

On the counter of the Republican Lyre is a machine where you put in a franc and a child's handful of peanuts comes out. Boris fed coin after coin into the machine and asked for a soup plate.

When the men standing at the bar raised their glasses of champagne and nodded towards Boris, they were each toasting the blond: and each was picturing himself in Boris's place, some with envy, and all with that odd nostalgia which every-one feels for what they know they will never live.

Beside Marc stood Jean, who had once been a long-distance lorry driver. Now he kept rabbits with his wife and was seventy. Jean was in the middle of a story:

Guy was pissed out of his mind, Jean was saying, Guy slumped down onto the floor and lay there flat out, as if he were dead. Jean paused and looked at the faces around the bar to emphasize the impasse. What should we do with him? It was then that Patrick had his idea. Bring him round to my place, said Patrick. They got Guy into the car and they drove him up to Patrick's. Bring him in here, lay him on the work-bench, said Patrick. Now slip off his trousers.

The blond put some nuts into Boris's mouth.

You're not going to harm him? Slip off his trousers, I tell you. Now his socks. There he lay on the workbench, as naked as we'll all be when the Great Holiday starts. What now? He's broken his leg, announced Patrick. Don't be daft. We're going to make him believe he broke his leg, Patrick explained. Why should he believe it? Wait and see. Patrick mixed up a bathful of plaster and, as professionally as you'd expect from Patrick, he plastered Guy's leg from the ankle to halfway up the thigh. Jean paused to look round at his listeners. On the way home in the car Guy came round. Don't worry, mate, said Patrick, you broke your leg, but it's not bad, we took you to the hospital and they've set it in plaster and they said you could have it off in a week, it's not a bad fracture. Guy looked down at his leg and the tears ran down his cheeks. What a cunt I am! he kept repeating. What a cunt I am!

What happened afterwards? Marc asked.

He was a week off work, watching TV, with his leg up on a chair!

The blond began to laugh and Boris put the back of his

hand against her throat—for fear that the palm was too calloused—and there he could feel the laughter, which began between her hips, gushing up to her mouth. Systematically he moved the back of his immense hand up and down the blond's throat.

Jean, the lorry driver who now kept rabbits, watched this action, fascinated, as if it were more improbable than the story he had just told.

I couldn't believe it, he recounted to the habitués of the Republican Lyre later that night: there was Boris, over there, bone-headed Boris caressing the blond like she was a sitting squirrel, and feeding her nuts from a soup plate. And what do you think he does when the husband comes in? He stands up, holds out his hand to the husband and announces: What do you want to drink? A white wine with cassis? I'm taking her to the ball tonight, Boris says. We shan't be back till morning.

The ball was in the next village. All night it seemed to Boris that the earth was moving past the plough of its own volition.

Once they stopped dancing to drink. He beer, and she lemonade.

I will give you the Mother's house, he said.

Why do you call it that?

My mother inherited it from her father.

And if one day you want to sell it?

How can I sell it if I've given it to you?

Gérard will never believe it.

About our child?

No. About the house, he won't agree to move in, unless it's certain.

Leave Gérard! Come and live with me.

No, Humpback, I'm not made for preparing mash for chickens.

Once again, by way of reply, Boris thrust his massive head against her breast. His face fitted into her breast like a gun into its case lined with velvet. For how long was his face buried there? When he raised it he said: I'll give you the house formally, I'll see the notary, it'll be yours, yours not his, and then it'll go to our child. Do you want to dance again?

Yes, my love.

They danced until the white dress with red polka dots was stained with both their sweats, until there was no music left, until her blond hair smelled of his cows.

Years later, people asked: how was it possible that Boris, who never gave anything away in his life, Boris, who would cheat his own grandmother, Boris, who never kept his word, how was it that he gave the house to the blond? And the answer, which was an admission of the mystery, was always the same: a passion is a passion.

Women did not ask the same question. It was obvious to them that, given the right moment and circumstances, any man can be led. There was no mystery. And perhaps it was for this reason that the women felt a little more pity than the men for Boris.

As for Boris, he never asked himself: Why did I give her the house? He never regretted this decision, although—and here all the commentators are right—it was unlike any other he had ever taken. He regretted nothing. Regrets force one to relive the past, and, until the end, he was waiting.

The flowers which grew in the mountains had brighter, more intense colours than the same flowers growing on the plain; A similar principle applied to thunderstorms. Lightning in the mountains did not just fork, it danced in circles; the thunder did not just clap, it echoed. And sometimes the echoes were still echoing when the next clap came, so that the bellowing became continuous. All this was due to the metal deposits in the rocks. During a storm, the hardiest shepherd asked himself: What in God's name am I doing here? And next morning, when it was light, he might find signs of the visitations of which, fortunately, he had been largely ignorant the night before: holes in the earth, burned grass, smoking trees, dead cattle. At the end of the month of August there was such a thunderstorm.

Some of Boris's sheep were grazing just below the Rock of St. Antoine on the far slopes facing east. When sheep are frightened they climb, looking to heaven to save them; and so Boris's sheep moved up to the scree by the rock, and there they huddled together under the rain. Sixty sheep, each one resting his drenched head on the oily drenched rump or shoulders of his neighbour. When the lightning lit up the mountain—and everything appeared so clear and so close that the moment seemed endless—the sixty animals looked like a single giant sheepskin coat. There were even two sleeves, each consisting of half a dozen sheep, who were hemmed in along two narrow corridors of grass between the rising rocks. From this giant coat, during each lightning flash, a hundred or more eyes, glistening like brown coal, peered out in fear. They were right to be frightened. The storm centre was approaching. The next forked lightning struck the heart of the coat and the entire flock was killed. Most of them had their jaws and forelegs broken by the shock of the electrical discharge, received in the head and earthed through their thin bony legs.

In the space of one night Boris lost three million.

It was I, thirty-six hours later, who first noticed the crows circling in the sky. Something was dead there, but I didn't know what. Somebody told Boris, and the next day he went up to the Rock of St. Antoine. There he found the giant sheepskin coat, discarded, cold, covered with flies. The carcasses were too far from any road. The only thing he could do was burn them where they lay.

He fetched petrol and diesel oil and started to make a pyre, dragging the carcasses down the two sleeves and throwing them one on top of another. He started the fire with an old tyre. Thick smoke rose above the peak, and with it the smell of burned animal flesh. It takes very little to turn a mountain into a corner of hell. From time to time Boris consoled himself by thinking of the blond. Later he would laugh with her. Later, his face pressed against her, he would forget the shame of this scene. But more than these promises which he made to himself, it was the simple fact of her existence which encouraged him.

By now everybody in the village knew what had happened to Boris's sheep. No one blamed Boris outright—how could they? Yet there were those who hinted that a man couldn't lose so many animals at one go unless, in some way, he deserved it. Boris neglected his cattle. Boris did not pay his debts. Boris was having it off with a married woman. Providence was delivering him a warning.

They say Boris is burning his sheep, said the blond, you can see the smoke over the mountain.

Why don't we go and watch? suggested Gérard.

She made the excuse of a headache.

Come on, he said, it's a Saturday afternoon and the mountain air will clear your head. I've never seen a man burning sixty sheep.

I don't want to go.

What's the matter?

I'm worried.

You think he could change his mind about the house now?
He'll certainly be short of money.

A flock of sheep's not going to make him change his mind
about the house.

We shouldn't count our chickens—

Only one thing could make him go back on his word about
the house.

If you stopped seeing him?

Not exactly.

What then?

Nothing.

Has he mentioned the house recently?

Do you know what he calls it? He calls it the Mother's
house.

Why?

She shrugged her shoulders.

Come on, said Gérard.

Gérard and his wife drove up the mountain to where the
road stopped. From there, having locked the car, they continued on foot. Suddenly she screamed as a grouse flew up
from under her feet.

I thought it was a baby! she cried.

You must have drunk too much. How can a baby fly?

That's what I thought, I'm telling you.

Can you see the smoke? Gérard asked.

What is it that's hissing?

His sheep cooking! said Gérard.

Don't be funny.

Grasshoppers.

Can you smell anything?

No.

Imagine being up here in a storm! she said.

I've better things to do.

It's all very well for you to talk, you've never lifted a shovel in your life, she said.

That's because I'm not stupid.

No. Nobody could call you that. And he's stupid, Boris is stupid, stupid, stupid!

He was encouraging the fire with fuel, whose blue flames chased the slower yellow ones. He picked up a sheep by its legs, and swung it back and forth, before flinging it high into the air so that it landed on top of the pyre, where, for a few minutes longer, it was still recognizable as an animal. The tear-stains on his cheek were from tears provoked by the heat and, when the wind turned, by the acrid smoke. Every few minutes he picked up another carcass, swung it to gain momentum, and hurled it into the air. The boy who had never been able to tap the ash-bark gently enough had become the man who could burn his own herd single-handed.

Gérard and the blond stopped within fifty yards of the blaze. The heat, the stench and something unknown prevented them approaching further. This unknown united the two of them: wordlessly they were agreed about it. They raised their hands to protect their eyes. Fires and gigantic waterfalls have one thing in common. There is spray torn off the cascade by the wind, there are the flames: there is the rockface dripping and visibly eroding, there is the breaking up of what is being burned: there is the roar of the water, there is the terrible chatter of the fire. Yet at the centre of both fire and waterfall there is a persistent calm. And it is this calm which is cata-strophic.

Look at him, whispered Gérard.

Three million he's lost, poor sod! murmured the blond.

Why are you so sure he isn't insured?

I know, she hissed, that's why. I know.

Boris, his back to the fire, was bent over his haversack

drinking from a bottle of water. Having drunk, he poured water onto his face and his black arms. Its freshness made him think of how he would strip in the kitchen this evening and wash before going to visit the blond.

When Boris turned back towards the fire he saw them. Immediately a gust of smoke hid them from view. Not for a moment, however, did he ask himself whether he had been mistaken. He would recognize her instantly whatever she was doing, anywhere. He would recognize her in any country in the world in any decade of her life.

The wind veered and he saw them again. She stood there, Gérard's arm draped over her shoulders. It was impossible that they had not seen him and yet she made no sign. They were only fifty yards away. They were staring straight at him. And yet she made no sign.

If he walked into the fire would she cry out? Still holding the bottle, he walked upright, straight—like a soldier going to receive a medal—towards the fire. The wind changed again and they disappeared.

The next time the smoke cleared the couple were nowhere to be seen.

Contrary to what he had told himself earlier, Boris did not come down that night. He stayed by the fire. The flames had abated, his sheep were ashes, yet the rocks were still oven-hot and the embers, like his rage, changed colour in the wind.

Huddled under the rock, the Milky Way trailing its veil towards the south, he considered his position. Debts were warnings of the ultimate truth, they were signs, not yet insistent, of the final inhospitality of life on this earth. After midnight the wind dropped, and the rancid smell, clinging to the scree, was no longer wafted away; it filled the silence, as does the smell of cordite when the sound of the last shot has died away. On this inhospitable earth he had found, at the age of forty-one, a shelter. The blond was like a place: one where the law of inhospitality did not apply. He could take this place anywhere, and it was enough for him to think of her, for him to approach it. How then was it possible that she had come up the mountain on the day of his loss and not said a word? How was it possible that on this rock, far above the village, where even the church bells were inaudible, she should have come as close as fifty yards and not made a sign to him? He stirred the embers with his boot. He knew the answer to the question and it was elementary. He pissed into the fire and on the stones his urine turned into steam. It was elementary. She had come to watch him out of curiosity.

Before he saw her, he was telling himself that, after all, he had only lost half his sheep. As soon as he saw her with his own eyes, and she made no sign to him, his rage joined that of the fire: he and the fire, they would burn the whole world together, everything, sheep, livestock, houses, furniture, forests, cities. She had come out of curiosity to watch his humiliation.

All night he hated her. Just after sunrise, when it was coldest, his hatred reached its zenith. And so, four days later he was asking himself: could she have had another reason for coming up to the Rock of St. Antoine?

Boris decided to remain in the mountains. If he went down to the village, everyone would stare at him to see how he had taken his loss. They would ask him if he was insured, just in order to hear him say no. This would give them pleasure. If he went down he might start breaking things, the windows of the mayor's office, the glasses on the counter of the Republican Lyre, Gérard's face, the nose of the first man to put an arm round the blond's waist. The rest of his sheep were near Peniel, where there was a chalet he could sleep in. Until the snow came, he would stay there with his remaining sheep. Like that, he would be on the spot to bring them down for the winter. If she had really come to see him for another reason, she would come again.

A week passed. He had little to do. In the afternoons he lay on the grass, gazed up at the sky, occasionally gave an order to one of the dogs to turn some sheep, idly watched the valleys below. Each day the valleys appeared further away. At night he was obliged to light a fire in the chalet; there was no chimney but there was a hole in the roof. His physical energy was undiminished, but he stopped plotting and stopped desiring. On the mountainside opposite the chalet was a colony of marmots. He heard the marmot on guard whistle whenever one of his dogs approached the colony. In the early morning he saw them preparing for the winter and their long sleep. They lifted clumps of grass with roots attached, and carried them, as if they were flowers, to their underground hide-out. Like widows, he told himself, like widows.

One night, when the stars were as bright as in the spring, his anger returned to galvanize him. So they think Boris is finished, he muttered to the dogs, but they are fucking well wrong. Boris is only at the beginning. He slept with his fist in his mouth, and that night he dreamed.

The following afternoon he was lying on his back looking up at the sky, when suddenly he rolled over onto his stomach in order to look down the track which led through the forest to the tarred road. His hearing had become almost as acute as that of his dogs. He saw her walking towards him. She was wearing a white dress and blue sandals, around her neck a string of beads like pearls.

How are you, Humpback?

So you've come at last!

You disappeared! You disappeared! She opened her arms to embrace him. You disappeared and so I said to myself: I'll go and find Humpback, and here I am.

She stepped back to look at him. He had a beard, his hair was tangled, his skin was dirty and his blue eyes, staring, were focused a little too far away.

How did you get here? he asked.

I left the car at the chalet below.

Where the old lady is?

There's nobody there now, and the windows are boarded up.

They must have taken the cows down, he said. What date is it?

September 30th.

What did you come for, when I was burning the sheep?

How do you mean?

You came up to the Rock of St. Antoine with your husband.

No.

The day I was burning the sheep, I saw you.

It must have been somebody else.

I'd never mistake another woman for you.

I was very sorry to hear about what happened to your sheep, Boris.

Grandma used to say that dreams turned the truth upside down. Last night I dreamed we had a daughter, so in life it'll be a son.

Humpback, I'm not pregnant.

Is that true?

I don't want to lie to you.

Why did you come to spy on me? If you're telling the truth, tell it.

I didn't want to.

Why didn't you come over and speak to me?

I was frightened.

Of me?

No, Humpback, of what you were doing.

I was doing what had to be done. Then I was going to come and visit you.

I was waiting for you, she said.

No, you weren't. You had seen what you wanted to see.

I've come now.

If he's conceived today, he'll be born in June.

After these words, he roughly took her arm and led her towards the crooked chalet whose wood had been blackened by the sun. He pushed open the door with his foot. The room was large enough for four or five goats. On the earth floor were blankets. The window, no larger than a small transistor radio, was grey and opaque with dust. There was a cylinder of gas and a gas-ring, on which he placed a black saucepan with coffee in it.

I'll give you whatever you want, he said.

He stood there in the half light, his immense hands open. Behind him on the floor was a heap of old clothes, among which she recognised his American army cap and a red shirt which she had once ironed for him. In the far corner something scuffled and a lame lamb hobbled towards the door where a dog lay. The floor of beaten earth smelled of dust, animals and coffee grounds. Taking the saucepan off the gas, he turned down the flame, and its hissing stopped. The silence which followed was unlike any in the valley below.

If it's a boy, I'll buy him a horse—

Ignoring the bowl of coffee he was holding out to her, without waiting for the end of his sentence, she fled. He went to the door and watched her running, stumbling downhill. Occasionally she looked over her shoulder as if she thought she were being pursued. He did not stir from the doorway and she did not stop running.

In the evening it began to snow, tentatively and softly. Having brought all three dogs into the chalet, Boris bolted the door, as he never did, lay down beside the animals and tried to sleep, his fist in his mouth. The next morning, beneath the white pine trees and through the frozen brambles and puddles of water, he drove his flock of miserable grey sheep towards the road that led down to the village.

When Corneille the cattle dealer drew up in his lorry before Boris's house and walked with the slow strides of the fat man he was through the snow to tap on the kitchen window, Boris was not surprised; he knew why Corneille had come. He swore at his dogs, who were barking, threatened them with being salted and smoked if they were not quieter, and opened the door. Corneille, his hat tilted towards the back of his head, sat down on a chair.

It's a long time since we've seen you, said Corneille. You weren't even at the Fair of the Cold. How are things?

Quiet, replied Boris.

Do you know they are closing the abattoir at Saint-Denis? Everything has to be taken to A—— now.

I hadn't heard.

More and more inspections, more and more government officials. There's no room for skill anymore.

Skill! That's one way of naming it!

You've never been short of that sort of skill yourself, said Corneille. There I take my hat off to you!

In fact he kept his hat on and turned up the collar of his overcoat. The kitchen was cold and bare, as if it had shed its leaves like the beech trees outside, its leaves of small comfort.

I'll say this much, continued Corneille, nobody can teach me a new trick, I know them all, but there's not one I could

teach you either. All right, you've suffered bad luck, and not
only last month up on the mountain—The poor bugger Boris,
we said, how's he going to get out of this one?—you've
suffered bad luck, and you've never had enough liquid cash.

From his right-hand overcoat pocket he drew out a wad of
fifty-thousand notes and placed them on the edge of the table.
One of the dogs sniffed his hand. Fuck off! said Corneille,
pushing the dog with one of his immense thighs, the overcoat
draped over it so that it advanced like a wall.

I'm telling you, Boris, you could buy the hind legs off a
goat and sell them to a horse! And I mean that as a compli-
ment.

What do you want?

Aren't you going to offer me a glass? It's not very warm in
your kitchen.

Gnôle or red wine?

A little gnôle then. It has less effect on Old King Cole.

So they say.

I hear you swept her off her feet, said Corneille, and the
husband under the carpet!

Boris said nothing but poured from the bottle.

Not everyone could do that, said Corneille, that takes
some Old King Cole!

Do you think so? What are you showing me your money for?

To do a deal, Boris. A straight deal, for once, because I
know I can't trim you.

Do you know how you count, Corneille? You count one,
two, three, six, nine, twenty.

The two men laughed. The cold rose up like mist from the
stone floor. They emptied the little glasses in one go.

The winter's going to be long, said Corneille, the snow has
come to stay. A good five months of snow in store for us. That's
my prediction and your uncle Corneille knows his winters.

Boris refilled the glasses.

The price of hay is going to be three hundred a bale before Lent. How was your hay this year?

Happy!

Not your woman, my friend, your hay.

Happy, Boris repeated.

I see your horses are still out, said Corneille.

You have sharp eyes.

I'm getting old. Old King Cole is no longer the colt he once was. They tell me she's beautiful, with real class.

What do you want?

I've come to buy.

Do you know, said Boris, what the trees say when the axe comes into the forest?

Corneille tossed back his glass, without replying.

When the axe comes into the forest, the trees say: Look! The handle is one of us!

That's why I know I can't trim you, said Corneille.

How do you know I want to sell? Boris asked.

Any man in your position would want to sell. Everything depends upon the offer, and I'm going to mention a figure that will astound you.

Astound me!

Three million!

What are you buying for that? Hay?

Your happy hay! said Corneille, taking off his hat and putting it further back on his head. No. I'm willing to buy everything you have on four legs.

Did say ten million, Corneille?

Boris stared indifferently through the window at the snow.

Irrespective of their condition, my friend. I'm buying blind. Four million.

I've no interest in selling.

So be it, said Corneille. He leaned forward, his elbows on the table, like a cow getting up from the stable floor, rump first, forelegs second. Finally he was upright. He placed his hand over the pile of banknotes, as if they were a screaming mouth.

I heard of your troubles, he said very softly in the voice that people use in a sickroom. I have a soft spot for you, and so I said to myself, this is a time when he needs his friends and I can help him out. Five million.

You can have the horses for that.

Corneille stood with his hand gagging the pile of money.

If you take my offer, if you have no animals during the winter, my friend, you can sell your hay, you can repair the roof of your barn, and when the spring comes, you'll have more than enough to buy a new flock. Five million.

Take everything, said Boris. As you say, it's going to be a long winter. Take everything and leave the money on the table. Six million.

I don't even know how many sheep I'm buying, muttered Corneille.

On this earth, Corneille, we never know what we're buying. Perhaps there's another planet where all deals are straight. All I know is that here the earth is peopled by those whom God threw out as flawed.

Five and a half, said Corneille.

Six.

Corneille lifted his hand from the pile and shook Boris's hand.

Six it is. Count it.

Boris counted the notes.

If you want a tip from a very old King Cole, Corneille spoke evenly and slowly, if you want a tip, don't spend it all on her.

For that you'll have to wait and see, Corneille, just as I am going to do.

■ ■ ■

There followed the correspondence between Boris and the blond. This consisted of two letters. The first, with the postmark of October 30th, was from him:

My darling,
I have the money for our fares to Canada. I am waiting for you—

always your Boris.

The second, dated November 1st, was from her:

Dearest Humpback,
In another life I might come—in this one forgive Marie-Jeanne.

There were no longer any sheep to feed. The horses had gone from the snow-covered orchard. When the lorry had come to fetch them, there was half a bale of hay lying on the snow and Boris had thrown it into the lorry after his horses. On one small point Marc was right when he said that Boris died like one of his own beasts. Not having to feed his animals gave him the idea of not feeding himself.

In the icy trough in the yard he hid a bottle of champagne, ready to serve cold. The water detached the label and after a week it floated to the surface. When the police opened the kitchen cupboard, they found a large jar of cherries in eau-de-vie with a ribbon round it, and a box of After Eight chocolates, open but untouched. Most curious of all, on the kitchen floor beneath the curtainless windows, they found a confectioner's cardboard box with golden edges, and inside it were rose-pink sugared almonds such as are sometimes distributed to guests and friends after a baptism. On the floor too were blankets, dogshit and wet newspapers. But the dogs had not touched the sugared nuts.

In the house during the unceasing period of waiting he did not listen to the sounds which came from outside. His hearing was as unimpaired as is mine now, registering the noise of my pen on the paper—a noise which resembles that of a mouse at night earnestly eating what its little pointed muzzle has discovered between its paws. His hearing was unimpaired, but his indifference was such that the crow of a neighbour's cock, the sound of a car climbing the road from which one looks down onto the chimney of his house, the shouts of children, the drill of a chain-saw cutting in the forest beyond the river, the klaxon of the postman's van—all these sounds became nameless, containing no message, emptier, far emptier than silence.

If he was waiting and if he never lost for one moment, either awake or asleep, the image of what he was waiting for —the breast into which his face at last fitted—he no longer knew where it would come from. There was no path along which he could look. His heart was still under his left ribs, he still broke the bread into pieces for the dogs with his right hand, holding the loaf in his left, the sun in the late afternoon still went down behind the same mountain, but there were no longer any directions. The dogs knew how he was lost.

This is why he slept on the floor, why he never changed a garment, why he stopped talking to the dogs and only pulled them towards him or pushed them away with his fist.

In the barn when he climbed a ladder, he forgot the rope, and, looking down at the hay, he saw horses foaling. Yet considering his hunger, he had very few hallucinations. When he took off his boots to walk in the snow, he knew what he was doing.

One sunny day towards the end of December, he walked barefoot through the snow of the orchard in the direction of the stream, which marks the boundary of the village. It was there that he first saw the trees which had no snow on them.

The trees form a copse which I would be able to see now from the window, if it were not night. It is roughly triangular, with a linden tree at its apex. There is also a large oak. The other trees are ash, beech, sycamore. From where Boris was standing the sycamore was on the left. Despite the December afternoon sunlight, the interior of the copse looked dark and impenetrable. The fact that none of the trees were covered in snow appeared to him to be improbable but welcome.

He stood surveying the trees as he might have surveyed his sheep. It was there that he would find what he awaited. And his discovery of the place of arrival was itself a promise that his waiting would be rewarded. He walked slowly back to the house but the copse was still before his eyes. Night fell but he could still see the trees. In his sleep he approached them.

The next day he walked again through the orchard towards the stream. And, arms folded across his chest, he studied the copse. There was a clearing. It was less dark between the trees. In that clearing she would appear.

She had lost her name—as the champagne bottle which he was keeping for her arrival had lost its label. Her name was forgotten, but everything else about her his passion had preserved.

During the last days of the year, the clearing in the copse grew larger and larger. There was space and light around every tree. The more he suffered from pains in his body, the more certain he was that the moment of her arrival was approaching. On the second of January in the evening he entered the copse.

During the night of the second, Boris's neighbours heard

his three dogs howling. Early next morning they tried the kitchen door, which was locked on the inside. Through the window they saw Boris's body on the floor, his head flung back, his mouth open. Nobody dared break in through the window for fear of the dogs, savagely bewailing the life that had ended.

So I have told the story. The wind is driving the powdered snow into deep drifts. Everything is being covered in white, even the air. If you walk across this wind, out in the fields away from the shelter of the village, it will line your cheeks with ice in one minute and the pain in your skull, if you stay there, will grow like a concussion after a blow.

Anyone who believes that evil does not exist and that the world was made good should go out tonight into the fields.

On a night like this a game of cards is like a bed dragged into the middle of the room. Four of us huddle together to play belote. The electricity has been cut. The two candles give just enough light to see the cards in our hands. La Patronne puts on her glasses. Sometimes she takes a torch out of her pocket to distinguish between a heart and a diamond.

THE
TIME
OF THE
COSMONAUTS

If every event which occurred could be given a name, there would be no need for stories. As things are here, life outstrips our vocabulary. A word is missing and so the story has to be told. What, for instance, was the relation between the old shepherd Marius and the baby in Danielle's womb when she left the village? Was he the child's godfather? Hardly.

The story began and ended in the summer of 1982, high up in the alpage which we call Peniel. Some say that they know the name Peniel comes from the bible. Genesis. Chapter 32. But if you read that, it won't really tell you what happened between Marius and Danielle.

Peniel is a plateau at an altitude of 1,600 metres. One edge of the plateau dominates, from a colossal rockface, the village below. From there, when there's a rainstorm and it's sunny, you can look down onto the top of a rainbow—as if it were the arch of a bridge at your feet. The rockface is mostly limestone, occasionally mixed with flysch. The other edges of the plateau are lost in the mountains beyond.

Once there was a forest on this plateau and some gigantic tree trunks are still preserved beneath a layer of clay, under the topsoil on which the pastures grow. Where this clay and the ancient forest are nearest to the surface, the earth is oily and damp, and on the rocks a dark green moss grows, which, if you touch it or lie down on it, feels like fur. This is how the rocks become like animals.

A number of years ago when the Russian, Gagarin, the first man in space, was circling the earth, every one of the twenty scattered chalets at Peniel housed, each summer, cattle and women and men. So many cattle that there was only just enough grass to go round. By common accord grazing time was limited. You got up at three to milk and you took the cows out to pasture as soon as it was light. At ten, when the sun was beginning to climb high in the sky, you brought them home and made your cheese. In the stable you gave them grass which you'd scythed at midday. After lunch you took a siesta. At four you milked again, and only then did you take the cows out a second time to pasture, and there you stayed with them until you could no longer see the trees but only the forest. You brought the cows back in and when they were bedded down on their straw, you could go outside and peer up into the night, where the Milky Way looked like gauze, and try to spot Gagarin in his circling Sputnik. All this was twenty-five years ago. During the summer in question—the summer of 1982—only two of the twenty chalets were inhabited, one by Marius and the other by Danielle, and there was so much grass they could let their animals graze night and day.

The two chalets are separated by a pass flanked by two peaks, the St. Pair and the Tête de Duet. It took Danielle half an hour to walk across the pass to Marius's chalet.

Why do he-goats smell so strongly? Marius asked her when she arrived the first time. After a winter of ice and snow you go into the stable and you know that last year there was a he-goat here! Rams don't smell like that, bulls don't smell like that, stallions don't smell like that, why do he-goats? The only other smell as strong as the smell of the he-goat, Marius continued, is the smell of a tannery. When I came back to the village, it took me six months to get that stench out of my skin. When I came back to the village, you could pluck a hair out of any part of my body—he fixed Danielle with his shrewd unflinching eyes so that what he meant should not escape her—any part of my body, sniff it, and say: this man has worked in a tannery.

What do you want a he-goat to be? replied Danielle, all he-goats have a strong smell, don't they?

Another thing—apart from the stench of the tannery—which Marius brought back with him to the village was his way of wearing a hat. He wore his hat pulled rakishly down over one eye. Like a boss. Not the boss of a factory but of a gang. And he was never without a hat. He slept with a hat on. When he brought in his cows after a storm—if the downpour is violent they refuse to budge, they put down their heads, they arrange their backs like roofs so the rain runs off either side, and they wait—when Marius brought in his herd after a storm and his hat was so drenched that even indoors it went on raining, he took it off and straightaway put on another.

Putting on a hat was for him a gesture of authority, and from the age of thirty to the age of seventy, the authority of the gesture had not changed. He wore his hat now as if he were expecting total obedience from thirty cows and one dog.

That's Violette there, he muttered to Danielle, pointing with his stick to a large brown cow with black eyes and horns. Always the last to come when called, always wandering off by herself, she has her own system, Violette, and I shall get rid of her in the autumn!

He had lost his father at the age of fourteen. His father, who married twice, had a passion for cards. Every evening in the winter he would say: *Sauva la graisse!* Wipe the grease off the table, we are going to play cards. And so he became known as Emilien à Sauva, and his son as Marius à Sauva.

Emilien, the father, left little behind except debts. The family house was sold, and Marius, who was the eldest son, had to leave to look for work in Paris. As he climbed for the first time in his life into a train, he swore that he would come back with enough money to pay off the family debts and that eventually he would have the largest herd of cows in the village.

So you're going to sweep their chimneys? asked the ticket collector.

I'll eat their shit, said Marius the boy, if they pay me more for it.

He achieved what he swore he would. He worked in a tannery in Aubervilliers, a little to the north of the Arc de Triomphe. By the time he was thirty he had paid off the family debts. By the time he was fifty he had the largest herd in the village.

They are calm today, Danielle, he went on, calm and agreeable, and they stay together. Not like yesterday—yesterday they could feel the storm, and there were flying ants. They ran with their tails straight out. They were as disagreeable as you can imagine yesterday. And today they are honeysweet. As sweet as honey, Danielle.

It was the beginning of the summer and the grass was full of flowers, vanilla orchids, arnica, red campion, globeflowers, and blue centaurea that people say are the souls of poets.

Danielle was twenty-three. Her mother was dead and she lived with her elderly father, who had five cows and some goats. She had a job in the warehouse of a furniture factory. But in the spring of '82 the factory went bankrupt, and so she proposed to take her father's animals to the mountains—to the chalet where she had spent several summers as a child with her mother.

How does she have the courage to stay up there alone? people in the village asked. Yet the truth was she didn't need courage. It suited her—the silence, the sun, the slow daily routine. Like many people who are sure of themselves, Danielle was a little intimidating. At village dances the boys didn't fall over themselves to partner her—though she danced well and had wide hips and tiny feet. They weren't sure she would laugh at their jokes. So they called her *slow*. In reality, this so-called slowness of hers was a kind of imperturbability. She had a wide face—a little like that of a Red Indian squaw—

with dark eyes, large shoulders, small wrists and plump capable hands. It was easy to imagine Danielle as the mother of several children—except that she seemed to be in no hurry to find a man to be their father.

Grandad! she teased Marius, when she paid him a second visit a few days later. You dye it, don't you?

Dye what?

Seventy and not a single white hair!

It's in the breeding.

Danielle looked away as if she had suddenly forgotten her joke. The few white clouds above the peaks were the only sign that the world was still going on.

My father had the same head of hair, Marius continued, thick and black as a lamb when they nailed him in his coffin. Go fetch Lorraine, Johnny! he called to the dog, Find Lorraine!

The dog bounded away to fetch a cow who was straying along the slope to the west. Over the seasons the cows at Peniel have made, with their own feet, narrow paths like terraces along the slopes. You can wander along one of those paths without really noticing that on one side the drop below is getting steeper and steeper.

Go fetch Lorraine!

Marius had his own way of calling. His calls sounded like an order and an appeal at the same time. Everyone discovers how to make their voice carry in the mountains, and everyone knows that animals respond to sounds which are like songs. Yet his shouts were not musical, they were a kind of convulsive cry and each phrase ended with the sound OVER! Johnny bring over! Take over! Over there Johnny over! Somebody suddenly awaking from sleep might cry out like Marius calling to his dog.

Fetch Lorraine over!

Dangerous, he said. Lilac fell there two years ago and broke a leg. To save the meat I had to hack the carcass with an axe and take the quarters back to the chalet on a sledge. Alone. No one to help and no one to see.

The next time Danielle paid him a visit was in the evening. It had been very hot all day, the goats were as languid as she was. When she had finished milking, she climbed up to the pass. There she could hear the bells of Marius's herd, and at the same time, behind her and much louder, the bells of her own five. She had an electric torch with her in case she needed it for the walk back.

Marius was sitting on a stool in his stable, empty except for one cow. He looked up from under his hat, his black eyes fixed intently upon Danielle.

I was doing my best to make you come, he growled, may need your help when it comes to pulling. I know my Comtesse.

Comtesse, the cow before them, had her tail in the air and glistening loops of mucus trailed from her distended vulva. Danielle approached her head and felt the temperature of her horns.

What she needs, she said, is some dew on her nose.

She wanted to joke because she saw that Marius's hands were trembling. How many calves had he delivered during his lifetime? And now he owned not one but thirty cows. Why should he be nervous? The last sunlight was shining between the slats of the west wall. When Comtesse moved her head the bell around her neck tolled like an animal in pain. It was stifling as though all the wood of the floor and walls and roof, all the wood of the stable, were feverish; Danielle knew why he was nervous. To be nervous like that he had to be a man and he had to be old: it wasn't the danger of losing the calf or the cow which worried him, it was a question of pride. As if he were being put to a test, as if he were on trial. No woman, young or old, would suffer like that.

The head's twisted, muttered Marius, pushing his hat further back on his head, that's why the bugger doesn't come. For the third or fourth time he rolled back his sleeve to the shoulder and plunged his right arm into the cow. The Comtesse was now so weak she was swaying like a drunk.

For Christ's sake hold her up, he shouted, do you want to break my arm? Hold her up! God almighty, it's not possible! Hold her up, do you hear me? Your father may be my worst enemy but you keep her on her feet, do you hear me?

Whilst he was shouting at Danielle he was quietly, systematically, searching with his open hand, fingers separated like probes, to find the calf's shoulders and then its haunches and then with a single hand to turn them so that the calf could engage the passage. He was sweating profusely, so were Danielle and the Comtesse. Mucus, wood impregnated with a century's smell of cows, sweat, and somewhere the iodine tang of birth.

It's done, he grunted. He withdrew his arm and almost immediately two front hooves appeared, forlorn-looking as drowned kittens. Danielle was fingering the rope, impatient to slip it round the hooves and pull, and so finish with a labour that had already gone on too long, yet she hesitated because Marius was standing there, his face a few inches from the cow's cunt, his eyes screwed up as if he were praying.

He's coming to us! He's coming. The calf slipped out limply, wearily, into Marius's arms. He poured eau-de-vie over his fingers and forced them into the calf's mouth so that it could suck. It looked more dead than alive. He carried it to the Comtesse, who licked its face and lowed. The sound she made was high and penetrating—a mad sound, thought Danielle. The calf stirred. She went to fetch some straw.

When all was arranged, Marius sat there on his stool, his right hand, with which he had turned the calf, still held open and extended, still making in the air of the stable the same gestures it had made in the womb. The difference was that it was no longer trembling.

You certainly know what you're doing, Grandad!

Not always, not always.

A sweet breeze was blowing through the open door. The light was fading in the stable.

I couldn't have done it without you, he said.

I did nothing.

He laughed and began to turn down the sleeves of his shirt. You were there! he cried, you were there! You kept her on her feet.

On her way home she was glad to have the torch, because the pass crosses from north to south, and with the moon still low in the east, the way between the crags was in dark shadow. She stopped to look up at the stars, which from there, where it was dark, seemed ten times brighter.

I often watched him. Toward midday I left my goats and climbed up the pass where there was a breeze, and there I ate my lunch. To be honest, I spied on him, for I was careful to remain hidden.

According to his children, who had left home, he was a tyrant. And what tyrannized them, apart from his orders, was his indefatigability.

Go fetch them over! Go take them over!

Every afternoon he had a different plan for where and how his herd should eat. He never left them in peace.

There were always jackdaws around the pass. When the sun was out and they were flying close to the rockface of St. Pair, their flying shadows were cast on the rock, and this seemed to double the number of birds in flight. Then, at a given moment, the leader of the flock would veer toward the sun, the others turning to follow, and their shadows would immediately vanish, so that it looked as if half the birds in flight had suddenly disappeared into thin air. Sometimes I lay there watching the birds appear and disappear until I lost all count of time. I would look down and notice Marius and his herd by the stream below where the cows drank at midday, and the next moment they were five kilometres away.

A week later Danielle visited Marius again. He was with his herd near the forest where two generations before some shepherds had mined for gold and found none.

Marius greeted her by saying: One day you'll be an old woman! Even you, Danielle! I had a fall last night.

So?

Everyone ages.

How did you fall?

By way of an answer, he started to undo his belt. His trousers, caked in mud and cowshit, drenched and dried in the sun a thousand times, were, as usual, unbuttoned in front. Now they fell to the ground around his ankles. He turned so that she could see the back of his thigh, where just under the buttock something sharp had jaggedly torn the flesh. His legs were as white as they must have been in the cradle.

Is it deep? he asked.

It needs cleaning.

It bled like a pig.

What did you put on it?

Some brandy and some arnica.

It needs washing and bandaging, she said.

What is it like?

It's about ten centimetres long and it's red like a wound.

Is it ugly? It's just where I can't see it.

It'll heal so long as you keep it clean.

Everything heals unless you die from it!

There were flies all round the brim of his hat.

Let's go to the chalet, she said.

The bowl from which he had drunk his coffee and eaten his bread was still on the kitchen table.

Living by myself, I don't have to change the plates, he said.

Where did you fall?

Out there where the woodpile is. Every night I cut the kindling wood to start the fire next morning. I must have tripped, I don't know how.

You do too much, Grandad.

Who else is going to do it? Do you know how many cheeses I make a week?

She shook her head.

Thirty.

You've got a son down below.

He's only interested in becoming mayor.

He'll never get elected.

I'll make you some coffee. He plugged in an electric coffee grinder. I couldn't manage without electricity, he said, electricity can replace a wife! He winked. A grotesque, undisguised wink.

She sipped the coffee. A few drops of rain began to fall. Within a minute the rain was beating on the roof like a drunk, and there were claps of thunder.

You're not frightened, Danielle?

She repeated what she'd often heard said: there are three sorts of lightning—the lightning of rain, the lightning of stone, and the lightning of fire—and there's nothing you can do about any of them.

The cows won't move in rain like this, he said.

When the thunder was further away, she said: If you lie down, I'll clean your leg.

The chalet, apart from the hayloft and stable, consisted of two rooms, one without a window for storing the cheeses, and one with a window for everything else. The bed, in the opposite corner from the stove, was made of wood and was screwed to the wall. He climbed up onto it, handed her a bottle of eau-de-vie, turned his back and lowered his trousers. Pinned to the planks of the wall beside the bed was a colour photo, torn from a magazine, of a large political demonstration by the Arc de Triomphe. She poured some eau-de-vie onto a cloth and began cleaning around the wound.

Crowds there that day, she said, looking at the photo.

I cut it out because I knew the Arc de Triomphe, he replied, I knew it well.

As a young man, she thought as she took hold of his leg, which was as pale as a baby's, he must have been unusually handsome, with his dark eyes, his thick eyebrows, and his jet-black moustache. In Paris he couldn't have lacked offers from women. Yet if he was to remain faithful to his oath, he could not afford to marry—whatever else he may have done—a seamstress or a florist. He had to find a wife who could milk the cows he was going to buy.

He clenched one fist.

Am I hurting you?

Hurting me? Do you know what happened to Jesus? Jesus was nailed to the cross, with nails through his hands and through his feet, right into the wood. That is how he was hurt. And he wasn't a sinner like me!

He didn't marry until he came back to the village. Elaine, his wife, died young and the day after her funeral he bought a milking machine.

Danielle poured a little eau-de-vie into the wound, and

then she took the new cheesecloth that he had given her and began to bandage the thigh. In order to do so she had to bend over him and pass her hand several times between his legs near his scrotum, and each time she did this she shut her eyes out of respect.

I would like to go to Paris, she said whilst bandaging him. Up to now I've never had the chance.

Just wait a little longer, Danielle, you're still a young woman and one day you'll go to Paris and Rome and New York, I daresay. People fly everywhere now. You'll see everything.

He swung his legs off the bed and winced a little.

Is it too tight?

Perfect.

He pulled up his trousers from his ankles and fastened his belt. He had kept his hat and boots on throughout the operation.

The storm was over and everything was washed and dust-free. Even the air. The valleys below, leading to the snow-capped mountains in the east, looked as if they had been painted by a miniaturist thousands of years before. By contrast, the rocks with moss, the grass and pine trees at Peniel looked new, as if just created. Marius's mood had changed with the atmospheric pressure and his eyes were full of laughter.

Come and help me bring the herd in! he said. No, don't protest, you can leave us at Nîmes and cut across by the arolle tree to the pass.

They walked with the dog along the edge of the pine forest. At one moment Danielle left the old man to make a detour to a hollow where you can find mushrooms called the Wolf's Balls. They are only good to eat when young. When old they turn to dust.

As she rejoined him, Marius said: You are as fearless as a ghost, Danielle.

A pity, she replied, ghosts aren't happy.

Happiness! He spoke the word as if it were the name of another of his disagreeable cows, like Violette. Happiness! Fetch them over! Bring Marquise over!

Nobody is happy, he announced. There are only happy moments. Like this one now with you.

The herd was easy to assemble that evening and the two of them had no more to do than follow the cows, who were going home fast, their necks moving up and down like pump handles and their bells ringing wildly. It must have been the massed bells which put the idea of glory into Marius's head. Glory doesn't last! he shouted. But he shouted it laughing, waving his stick to the music. Glory never lasts!

On her way home, Danielle turned around. Marius had put his hat on his stick and was waving it above his head in wide circles. She waved back and continued waving until she disappeared behind the last boulder.

In the afternoon when the cows were chewing the cud, Marius would lie down on the grass, take a newspaper from his pocket, read it for ten minutes, and then fall asleep. I had noticed this several times when I was spying on him from the pass at St. Pair. One day I visited him whilst he was sleeping. As I approached I made a bet with myself that I would take the newspaper out of his hand without waking him. The difficulty was going to be the dog. I would have to deal with Johnny.

The two of them were side by side, sheltered from the sun by sweetbriar bushes. The dog was wagging his tail, and I beckoned him to come. The old man was still asleep. He was

on his side, his knees slightly drawn up, his hat over his ear.
His head rested on a stone covered with moss. In his throat
Johnny was moaning a little with pleasure. I gave him my
sleeve to bite on. One of his hands lay, palm uppermost, on
the grass—he had unexpectedly long fingernails. The newspaper was against his stomach where his belt held up his
gaping trousers.

All the cows were lying down. There was no chorus of
bells for they were too still. Just one bell rang, as one cow
slowly turned her head, followed, after a pause, by another.
It was as if everything had slowed down like the old man's
pulse whilst he slept. I bent down and took his newspaper.
It was easy. I had won my bet. Now why should I wake him?
So I left the paper on the grass and very lightly I touched his
open hand because I did not want to leave furtively. I touched
his palm with my fingers, as lightly as if with a feather.

Why don't you get a husband? Marius asked Danielle the next
time she visited him.

I'm in no hurry.

You won't marry a boy from the village.

Why shouldn't I?

Because you are too independent.

Is that a fault?

Not if you have enough money!

I shan't get rich looking after Papa's goats.

That's not your job in life.

Are you saying I'm lazy?

No. I have a considerable admiration for you. The old man
spoke formally as if making a speech. A considerable admiration for you, Danielle. You are clever and you are thoughtful
—you let sleeping men lie!

It was then that she knew he had been feigning sleep. He must have felt it when she touched his hand. And he knew that she knew, but they did not speak of it.

So the weeks passed and so they learnt more about each other.

One night at the end of July a little before dawn when it was still dark, a car drove uphill, over the grass, towards the Tête de Duet and stopped a hundred metres away from Danielle's chalet. The car was a 1960 Mercedes Berlin-18, and it had been painted silver grey with a brush, not a spray gun. Six men got out of the car, each with a sack. They were careful not to slam the doors. The eldest, who wore a beret and a leather waistcoat, placed a huge hand around the neck of the youngest, who was yawning.

All the best things in life before you, boy!

Cut it out!

Do you see that peak? No, not that one. The one with snow on it, that's where we're felling today.

Christ! It's a good ten kilometres away.

The other five burst out laughing. Once again the boy had been taken in. Because it was early and the air was cold, laughing made some of them cough.

And it was this coughing which woke up Danielle. By the time she got out of bed and pulled on a skirt, all she could see from the door in the first light was an Indian file of men with sacks over their shoulders climbing towards the forest at St. Pair, and, before the chalet where her goats grazed, the shadowy silhouette of a car.

Later she tried each of the car's four doors. They were

locked. Through the windows, which looked bullet-proof, she admired the leather upholstery and the wooden dashboard of teak, with its dials like those on instruments made specially for doctors.

Afternoons she let the rabbits out of their cage. That day, after they had eaten, they hopped under the Mercedes, happy to find shade there. When she half-shut her eyes the rising heat waves along the ridges of the mountains opposite formed a blue halo. All day she heard the drone of the wood-cutters' chain saws.

In the evening, through the little window of the chalet, she watched the same six men with sacks over their shoulders coming down from St. Pair. The light was already fading. They were walking slowly, as if they were blind and were forced with each step to feel their way forward with their feet. They had a dog with them whose antics they were too tired to notice. Slowly they approached the chalet, each walking at his own speed, exhausted and alone.

When they saw her in the doorway, they became a little jauntier. The first sight of a woman—with the prospect of nine hours' respite from their backbreaking work—was a reminder of the other sweet side of the world.

I heard your saws.

Forty heads, miss.

Father's the one who counts, said a thickset one with sawdust in his hair. They all laughed and then fell shy.

You think it'll rain? one of them asked.

No, the birds are flying high.

Not tomorrow.

Forty!

Forty of 'em, shining like fish!

We strip 'em as we fell 'em.

It's steep, your Pair.

Pair? That's how you call it? asked the thickset one with sawdust in his hair.

St. Pair, she said.

Everywhere, on their arms, faces, vests, shoulders, they were smeared with a grey dust stuck to sweat and resin. This covering was so thick that in the half-light it looked as if their faces were covered with fur.

Steep and hot, said the boy.

In the trough there's running water, she said.

The men turned to look where she was pointing. A little distance from the chalet was a massive, scooped-out tree trunk, placed horizontally on some stones. In front of it waddled four geese, phosphorescent in the half-light, and above the trough was a water pipe which came directly out of the grassy mountainside behind.

It's a spring . . . if you want to wash.

We'll be home in twenty minutes, said the one they called Father, who wore a beret and a leather waistcoat.

Home?

The geese came towards the house in single file, breasts stuck out.

We're sleeping in the Chalet Blanc, explained Father.

There's no spring there, she said, only rainwater.

We've got jerry-cans.

Wash there, it's a spring, she said, a spring that never stops. You got soap?

Sure—and pyjamas! said a tall one.

In that case, I'll get you some.

She went inside. When she came out she handed a large cube of soap to Father. The men left their sacks on the ground and went over to the trough, which was long enough for them to stand side by side.

In the early night breeze she could smell the smell of their washing: a mixture of soap, stale shirts, petrol, smoke, pine resin, sweat. She observed them, stripped to the waist. The backs of the younger ones were suntanned. The elder ones always wore vests and their backs, in contrast to their arms and shoulders, were white. The Father had taken off his beret. They were throwing the soap to one another and laughing. They found the two brushes she kept there for scrubbing the churn. A woman, she thought, washes herself quite differently from a man; a man washes his body like he washes down a wheelbarrow; it's not by washing himself that a man learns to caress.

By the time they had put on their shirts it was dark. Under the eyes of Father each of them solemnly shook Danielle's hand, thanked her, and pronounced his name. The name she remembered was that of the thickset one with sawdust in his hair. When he arrived he was the dirtiest, and she sensed that this was because he worked the most ferociously. Pasquale was his name.

They dumped their sacks in the trunk of the Mercedes. Four got in behind. Father sat in the front, and Pasquale was the driver. He sat behind the wheel, hunched up, concentrated and impossible to distract.

Every night on their way home the woodcutters stopped to wash themselves in the trough by Danielle's chalet. She prepared coffee. They drank it outside sitting on their sacks. Virginio, who was tall and wore glasses, left a razor behind so that he could shave if he wanted. Danielle found a piece of broken mirror which she hung on a wire by the trough. She learnt that five of them came from the same village on the other side of the Alps, near Bergamo. Alberto came from Sicily. Every winter they returned home. She learnt that they were paid by the cubic metre of wood felled: the harder they worked, the quicker they earned. Father did the cooking. The Mercedes belonged to Pasquale.

Sometimes, when they passed in the very early morning they left a present for her: a tin of peaches, a bottle of vermouth. Once they left a scarf with a design of roses printed on it.

The first time I saw Pasquale out of his work clothes was when he knocked on the door whilst I was drinking coffee one morning.

I don't work on Sunday, he said.

You deserve a day of rest.

To do what?

There was a long silence.

Once we worked on a Sunday and I had an accident.

What happened? I asked.

The trees were falling badly, one after the other. We weren't working fast enough. That's why we decided to work on Sunday.

Would you like some cider?

He shook his head.

Some eau-de-vie?

I'm not thirsty.

I'll whip you some cream, I said.

His thick lips smiled and he opened his enormous hands in a gesture of submission.

Tell me what happened while I whip the cream.

A long silence.

About the Sunday you worked? I prompted him.

The very first tree I had to strip had fallen badly. Where we were working was very steep, like here. Rocks everywhere. Crevices. Gulleys. I told myself I'd work toward the head, so as not to have to walk back along where I'd already stripped. They're as slippery as fish when you strip them. Sometimes the resin splashes your face when you are axing the bark off.

The cream was thickening, leaving the side of the bowl. I watched Pasquale talking. There was a sadness in his face. He had stopped his story. Silence.

Do you have a brother or sister? I asked.

Not one. My mother died when I was born.

And your father?

He went to America and we never heard from him. He disappeared into America like a tear into a well, my aunt says.

Again silence—only the noise of my fork in the bowl.

Go on, I said, go on.

I started stripping her from the top and she began to roll from the head. Nothing stops a rolling tree except another tree or a rock. I hesitated because I was worried about the machine. It was a new one we had just bought. If you hesitate, you're lost. I jumped too late, holding the machine above my head. In the gulley I began to slide, it was as steep as the side of a pyramid. I slid over onto some dry rocks below and they broke a leg.

Could you get up?

The machine wasn't hurt!

No machine is worth a broken leg.

A machine like that costs half a million.

A long silence.

You couldn't get up?

They carried me home to the hut and laid me on the bed. Father said: Pasquale, can you wait till tomorrow? At first I didn't understand. Wait for what? Before we take you to hospital. That's twenty-four hours, I said. I'll sit with you, he replied, pain gets worse when you're alone. No, go back and work, I told him. Next day, Monday, they took me to hospital.

I handed him the bowl and he began to eat the cream. His huge hands rested on the table. To eat he lowered his head to the spoon. When he had finished he screwed up his face and smiled.

I've never tasted cream as good as that, he said.

Why didn't they take you to hospital immediately?

Because it was Sunday.

Well?

On Sundays we are not insured. What we do on Sundays is at our own risk. He looked at me very seriously. Like what we do today, he said.

There was another long silence and we did nothing.

If you come next Sunday with your friends, I said, I'll make a tart to go with the cream.

A few days later Danielle had the idea of passing by the arolle tree to get to the ridge above Nîmes—blueberries abound there—and then climbing down the scree to surprise Marius, whom she had neglected to visit for a week or two. She filled her bucket with berries and her fingers were stained blue as they used to be when she wrote in ink at school.

She approached the edge to look down on Peniel. The sky was cloudless. There was a strongish north wind which would fall when the sun went down. The sun was low in the sky so that the cows had long shadows like camels. Marius was there with his dog beside him. Yet there was something wrong. She sensed it without knowing why. The old man was shouting, his arms outstretched before him towards the crags. Why didn't the dog move? She couldn't hear what he was shouting because she was upwind. Then, abruptly, the wind dropped.

Sounds, like distances, are deceptive in the mountains. Sometimes you can recognise a voice, but not the words the voice is saying. Sometimes you hear a cow growl like a dog, and a whole flock of sheep singing like women. What Danielle thought she heard was:

Marius à Sauva! Marius à Sauva!

The sun was so low that it was lighting only one side of each mountain, one side of each forest, one side of each little hillock in the pastures; the other side of everything was in dark shadow, as if the sun had already set or not yet risen.

Perhaps he was telling the dog to go and save one of the cows, she argued to herself, that could sound like *à Sauva*. Yet why didn't the dog move?

Marius à Sauva!

She could no longer be sure, the wind had got up again. She picked her way carefully down the scree. Occasionally she dislodged a stone or a pebble which, clattering down, dislodged others, and they in their turn others. Yet despite the noise of her descent, Marius never once glanced up. It was as if at Nîmes, that evening, all sounds were playing tricks.

The dog ran to greet her. She waited for Marius to kiss her on her cheek as he always did. He kissed her and began talking as if they had been stopped in the middle of a conversation.

You see Guste over there—he pointed at a thickset Charolais with curly hair like wool—he's charming, Guste, the gentlest bull I've had, and already he's too old. I shall sell him for meat this autumn. He's two and a half. Next year his calves will be too small.

You must have thought I'd disappeared, Danielle said.

He lifted his hat and put it lower on his brow.

No, no, he said, gently. I hear their chain saws all day. And there are six of them, aren't there? Bring the Comtesse over! Gently, in God's name! Over!

He stopped in his tracks and leant against the side of a large boulder covered with moss. He was rubbing the back of his hand against the moss. And our summer at Peniel, he said, you'll remember it, won't you, Danielle?

The following Sunday the woodcutters came after supper to eat the blueberry tart Danielle had made. With them they brought two bottles of Italian sparkling wine. They were dressed as if they were going to town. Thin pointed shoes instead of boots, white shirts, natty belts. It was only their scarred hands they could do nothing about. Virginio was the most transformed by his change of clothes: tall and with glasses, he almost had the air of a schoolmaster. Father looked older, and Pasquale younger.

The days were drawing in and the end of the summer approaching. The pastures now were not green but lion-coloured, there were no flowers left, every day the buzzards circled lower, and by eight o'clock in the evening it was almost dark.

The men lay on the grass and looked up at the sky, where the first stars were appearing. They could feel the warmth of the earth through their shirts.

Would you like some more tart?

It was so good.

I made two, replied Danielle proudly and went indoors to fetch the second.

Next week the helicopter, said Virginio.

I've never seen a helicopter getting out the wood, said the boy.

Lifts pines like matches.

You look up and you feel as small as a frog, said Alberto the Sicilian.

Do you know how much it costs them to hire a helicopter for an hour?

No idea.

Two hundred thousand. In an hour it uses two hundred litres of petrol.

Here, Pasquale, take your tart, said Danielle. The other men were scarcely visible but she recognised their voices.

Helicopter pilot killed himself near Boege last year.

They were passing round a wine bottle.

Forgot his cables, didn't look down.

They're forbidden by law to do more than four hours' flying a day, said Father. In four hours they can get eighty trees off a mountain.

If one of his cables gets entangled, said Alberto, miming with his hands, it pulls him out of the sky. Plouff!

Next century we'll do everything in the sky, said the boy. Nobody'll work like us, next century.

Pasquale's packing it in next year, isn't that right?

I haven't decided yet, said Pasquale.

You won't make it. You can't take on the supermarkets single-handed, said Virginio.

With fruit and vegetables you can, insisted Pasquale.

No, said Father, you can't compete with their prices or their publicity.

I'm going to make my own publicity!

The other men laughed. A jet airliner crossed the sky, they could see its lights.

I'm going to get a bird, a Blue Rock Thrush.

He's out of his mind, our Pasquale!

You can teach a Blue Rock Thrush to talk.

So?

Every time a customer comes into the shop the bird'll talk. Pasquale recited a saleman's patter which, under the stars, sounded more like a prayer:

Guarda quanto è bella 'sta mela
quanto è bellissima e cotta!

Turning to Danielle, he translated the words for her: Look at the lovely apples, ripe and lovely apples!

The boy giggled. A good idea, said Father, but you need to give it a twist, make it unforgettable. Teach your bird to insult your customers. *Stronzo!* for the husband! *Fica* for the wife. They'll adore it, they'll adore it in Bergamo.

Are you sure?

I'll train the bird for you, said the Sicilian.

The moon was rising to the right of St. Pair. They watched a pink halo slowly changing into a white mist and then, suddenly, the bone-white incandescence of the first segment of the moon. Danielle sat down on the grass beside Pasquale.

When are you going to pack it in, Father?

Next year, sometime, never, sometime . . . I've no choice, I don't want to drop dead.

The head of the moon was now free in the sky, enormous and close-up like everything newborn.

Do you know who dropped dead last Tuesday? asked Virginio. Our friend Bergamelli—had his throat cut in prison.

Who did it?

The Brigade Rouge.

Bastards!

Bergamelli? Danielle whispered.

A gangster from Marseille . . . Virginio knew him when he was in prison, said Pasquale.

In the moonlight which became brighter as the moon grew smaller, Danielle could see Virginio's face, pillowed on his arms, gazing into the firmament.

He reminded me of my father, Virginio went on, Bergamelli had the same truculence, the same dark look when he was crossed, the same smile when something pleased him . . . He was killed when I was twelve, fell off a roof, my father.

Virginio took off his glasses and stared at the moon.

He was a mason, your father?

He built chimneys . . . The day they carried him home, I opened the veins on my wrists . . . they found me too soon. They carted me off to hospital, him down to the cemetery.

Shit! muttered Alberto.

From that day on I knew something, said Virginio; in this godforsaken life everyone is abandoned sooner or later. Father did everything with me. He taught me to cook, he showed me how to catch frogs, hundreds a night, he saw to it I knew how to pick locks, he was my music teacher, he told me about women, when he got drunk in the café by the big fountain he stood me on the table and I danced whilst he sang—and then one Wednesday morning, dry weather, sober week, clean shirt, good boots, one godforsaken Wednesday morning—pfft! like that, he fell off a roof. I used to go and look at the mark on the pavement where he landed.

From the stable came the muffled sound of goat bells. Sometimes at night their bells sound oleaginous, like the light on the surface of water in a deep well.

I can see him up there. He can't see us. If we all shouted together he wouldn't hear us. The dead are deaf to all the dynamite of the world.

A long silence followed, as if each one of them were thinking about the deafness of the dead.

It's hard to lose a father, said the Sicilian.

Harder than losing a mother?

When you lose your father you know there'll be no more miracles.

I never knew any miracles, said Pasquale beside Danielle on the grass, My father disappeared like a stone into a well before I knew him . . . so I never knew that loss.

The galaxies were visible at Peniel, as they never are on the plain. More than alcohol their silence makes people talk.

Is your father alive, Danielle? asked the boy.

He's alive . . . I don't know him like Virginio knew his
father. He doesn't talk to me much. All he says to me is: You'll
never make a wife, Danielle, like your mother was, you're
not modest enough to make a man happy, my girl.

Perhaps your Papa doesn't see you as you are, said Pasquale,
as if each of his words were a button he was pushing through
a buttonhole.

Pasquale should know, declared Virginio, suddenly jubilant,
for our Pasquale has eyes only for you!

The men, except Pasquale, laughed and the boy chanted:

> *Guarda quanto è bella 'sta mela*
> *quanto è bellissima e cotta!*

A few days later I climbed up to the pass with the idea of
paying Marius a visit. I looked down and saw his herd grazing by the stream. Then I heard his voice.

Marius à Sauva!

This time there was no doubt. Each syllable was distinct
and each syllable could be heard twice as it echoed off the
Tête de Duet. I crouched down on the ground and protected
my head with my arms as you do when lightning is near. Let
no more words be said, I prayed. Let him be quiet.

Marius à Sauva!

I crept forward on my stomach. He was standing by the
first boulder below. His arms were outstretched.

For your slope I have legs! he shouted.

The words still sounded like an order. What did he expect
to happen? What did he hope to see change among the crags?

For your slope I have my old legs!

The first time he had said nothing about his age. Now he was shouting about being old.

For your peak I have eyes!

He covered his eyes with his hands as if weeping.

The echo of each word made the silence which followed more terrible.

For your trees I have arms!

It would have been like a reply if something had moved. Everything remained motionless. Even I was holding my breath.

For your trees, my faithful arms!

Johnny was standing a little distance away from Marius, his tail between his legs.

For your load I have a back!

Not even the shape of a cloud changed. The old man was on his knees, looking up at the rockface.

For braking your sledge I have heels!

He was banging his feet on the earth and leaning his weight backwards as if bringing a charged sledge down a slope.

For braking your sledge I have heels and buttocks!

The cows were grazing peacefully behind him.

He climbed up on a boulder and stood on top of it, a good two metres above the ground. The sight of his tiny figure on the boulder dwarfed by the vast slopes of Peniel made me understand something. Marius was speaking of his achievement. Marius set no great store on the opinion of others. What Marius had done all his life he had done for its own sake. His achievement wasn't only his herd of thirty cows. It was also his will. Every day now, old and alone, he found an answer to the question Why go on? Nobody ever replied for him. Every day of the summer he had found the answer himself. And now, alone, he was boasting of it. That is what I told myself.

He thrust his hands into his trousers.

For your grot I have balls! For your grot my balls!

In the grass were autumn crocuses, their yellow and violet petals open like the beaks of baby birds. I smashed them with my fist. I smashed every one I could see.

When the woodcutters came to wash that evening, Danielle took Pasquale aside and said: I must talk to you.

Next Sunday, he said.

No! she insisted. Now! I can't stay another day if I don't talk to someone.

Pasquale went over to the trough and conferred with Father. She heard them speaking in Italian. Within five minutes Father was chivying the others to get a move on. The ritual of combing their hair one by one before the broken bit of mirror was renounced. They picked up their sacks, said good-bye, and with the slow list of their habitual fatigue, made their way to the car. Alberto the Sicilian got into the driver's seat.

Pasquale stayed behind and started shaving in front of the broken mirror.

You can't see a thing, Danielle said. Why do you have to shave now?

It's the first time you've asked me to supper.

Supper, it's only soup!

She began to sob silently. At first, peering into the mirror in which he could see nothing, Pasquale did not notice. It was her immobility which finally made him look up in her direction. He saw her shoulders trembling.

Shhh, he said, ssshhh. He walked her toward the chalet. A goose followed them. The door was open. Inside he stopped because it was pitch-dark and he could see nothing. She led him by the hand to a chair pulled up by the table, then she sat down herself on the chair opposite. She thought neither of lighting the lamp nor of heating the soup.

Something happened this afternoon, she said.

What?

In the pitch darkness, her hands placed on the table, she told him, quietly and slowly. She even told him about the crocuses. When she had finished there was silence. They heard a cow pissing in the stable, separated from the kitchen by a wall of pine boards.

Why should an old man talk to the mountains like that? she whispered.

Danielle, said Pasquale speaking very slowly and weighing each word, it was not to the mountains the old man was shouting, it was not to the mountains he was offering himself part by part, it was to you and you know that, you know that, don't you?

She began to sob again and the sobs became howls. She stood up to take in breath and to howl louder. Pasquale felt his way round the table and took her in his arms. She pressed her face as hard as she could against his chest. She bit his shirt which tasted of resin and sweat. She bit a hole in it.

On his wrist Pasquale had a watch with an alarm. It woke him at four-thirty. He did not want the others to pass by the chalet to fetch him, for he knew she would not yet understand their laughter. He kissed her repeatedly, he felt for his boots and clothes on the floor, and he slipped out to dress on the grass where they always left the Mercedes.

■　■　■

If today you pass through Bergamo and take the road north towards Zogno, you will find at the edge of the town where the sidewalk is no longer paved and the telegraph poles border the road, opposite an AGIP garage, next to a yard where men repair tyres, a shop with a sign that says VERDURA E ALIMENTARI. If it's winter you will find Pasquale inside serving. He weighs the vegetables on the scales with the scrupulousness and precision of Saint Peter. He looks preoccupied and proud.

Danielle's baby was a girl whom they christened Barbara. In the waste-land behind the shop, Pasquale has fixed a swing on a plane tree and Barbara sometimes plays there with her friends. The men in the tyre yard call Barbara their *Uccellina*, their tiny bird.

If it's summer you will not see Pasquale, for having spent all his savings on the shop, he's obliged once again to work as a woodcutter in the mountains on the other side of the frontier. When he's away he writes to Danielle most Sundays, telling her how many trees they've felled and what the weather is like. Danielle speaks Italian to her customers in the shop but with a noticeable French accent. She is more smartly dressed than many of them and wears large goldcoloured rings in her ears. She is expecting another baby.

Hanging on a wall near the door is a cage. The bird in it is blackish, a Blue Rock Thrush with a yellow beak and eyes like sequins. Whenever a customer comes into the shop the Blue Rock Thrush croaks out one of the insults Pasquale taught him. He is able to distinguish between men and women so that the insult fits. The customers would miss him by now if he weren't there. Sometimes a customer speaks back to the bird as if to a fellow sufferer, cursing men or women or the government or priests or lawyers or the tax office or the weather or the world. And sometimes when no one is paying him any attention or feeding him any nuts, he blinks his sequin eyes and slowly repeats a phrase which has the accent and cadence of another language, of the voice of another teacher.

Marius à Sauva! Marius à Sauva . . .

In the little grocery shop there's no question of sounds deceiving.

ONCE IN EUROPA

Before the poppy flowers, its green calyx is hard like the outer shell of an almond. One day this shell is split open. Three green shards fall to the earth. It is not an axe that splits it open, simply a screwed-up ball of membrane-thin folded petals like rags. As the rags unfold, their colour changes from neonate pink to the most brazen scarlet to be found in the fields. It is as if the force that split the calyx were the need of this red to become visible and to be seen."

The first sounds I remember are the factory siren and the noise of the river. The siren was very rare and probably that's why I remember it: they only sounded it in case of an accident. It was always followed by shouts and the sound of men running. The noise of the river I remember because it was present all the while. It was louder in the spring, it was quieter in August, but it never stopped. During the summer with the windows open you could hear it in the house; in the winter, after Father had put up the double windows, you couldn't hear it indoors, but you heard it as soon as you went outside to have a shit or to fetch some wood for the stove. When I went to school I walked beside the sound of the river.

At school we learnt to draw a map of the valley with the river coloured in blue. It was never blue. Sometimes the Giffre was the colour of bran, sometimes it was grey like a mole, sometimes it was milky, and occasionally but very rarely, as rare as the siren for accidents, it was transparent, and you could see every stone on its bed.

Here there's only the sound of the wind in the sheet flapping above us.

Once my mother told me to look after my baby cousin,

Claire. She left us alone in the garden. I started hunting for snails and I forgot Claire as I followed the track down to the river behind the furnaces. When my mother came back she found my baby cousin alone in the cradle under the plum trees.

The eagle could have come! she screamed, and pecked her poor eyes out!

She ordered me to pick some nettles, and stood over me whilst I did so. I remember I tried to protect my fingers by pulling down the sleeves of my pullover to cover my hands. The bunch of nettles I'd picked lay on the bench beside the water tap outside the door, waiting for my father to return.

You have to punish Odile, my mother said to him when he arrived and she handed him a cloth to hold the nettles with. She pulled up my pinafore. I was wearing nothing underneath.

Father stood there, still as a post. Then, picking up the nettles, he held them under the tap and turned on the water.

Like this it'll hurt less, he said. Leave her to me.

My mother went indoors and my father flicked the water from the nettles onto my backside. Not a single nettle touched me. He saw to that.

I thought I would be frightened and I am not. Since he was a small boy he was a son I could trust. Christian never did crazy things like the others and he was always reassuring. He inherited a lot from his father. I'll never forget, for as long as I live, the time when he grew his first moustache. I couldn't help crying out, he looked so much like his father. Perhaps the craziest thing Christian has ever done, at least amongst the things I know about, is to bring me up here. You're sure you're ready, Mother? Yes, my boy, I answered. And he screwed up his face as if he were in pain. Perhaps he was laughing.

Three thousand metres above the earth—he said he could climb to five thousand, I don't know whether he was boasting—with nothing but air between us and what we can see below and I'm not frightened! The moment our feet left the ground, the wind was there. The wind is holding us up and I feel safe, I feel—I feel like a word in the breath of a voice.

There was a riddle I liked as a child: four point to the sky, four walk in the dew and four have food in them; all twelve make one—what is it?

A cow, answered Régis, my elder brother, sighing loudly to show he had already heard the riddle many times before.

Odile, how is it a cow? asked poor Emile, my younger brother. People would take advantage of Emile all his life. His laziness was not so much a sin as a sickness. Each time I was pleased that Emile couldn't remember the riddle; it offered me the chance of explaining.

A cow has two horns, two ears pointing up, four legs for walking on, and four teats!

Six teats! cried Régis.

Four with milk in them!

Mother encouraged Régis to work with the furnaces because she was worried about Emile; it was going to be difficult for Emile to find a job anywhere, and so it made more sense if Emile was the one to stay at home with Father.

Father was against any son of his working in the factory. Régis would do better to go to Paris like men had done as long as anyone could remember. Long before the Eiffel Tower, long before the Arc de Triomphe, long before factories, they had gone to Paris to stoke fires and to sweep chimneys, and in the spring they had come back, money in their wallets, proud of themselves! Nobody could be proud of working— there. Father pointed with his thumb out of the window.

Times change, Achille, you forget that.

Forget! First, they try to take our land, then they want our children. What for? To produce their manganese. What use is manganese to us?

When Father was out in the fields, Régis said: He doesn't know what a stupid old man he looks, Papa, leading his four miserable cows through a factory yard four times a day!

We're over the factory. When we veer to the north I can smell the fumes in its smoke.

One night I went out to lock up the chickens and I found Father by the pear tree staring up at the sky and the flames flicking out of the top of the tallest chimney stack, almost half as tall as the cliff face behind it.

Look, Odile, he whispered, look! It's like a black viper standing on its tail—can you see its tongue?

I can see the flames, Papa, some nights they're blue.

Venom! he said. Venom!

Whenever I went near the factory, I saw the dust. It was the colour of cow's liver, except that, instead of being wet and shiny, it was a dry kind of sand: it was like dried liver, pulverised into dust. The big shop was taller than any pine tree and when one of the furnaces was opened, the hot air as it rose would make a draught so that high up, by the topmost girders, a breeze would blow the dust off all the ledges and you'd see a trailing cloud like a red veil hiding the roofing. This dust astonished and fascinated me. It turned the hair of all the men who didn't wear hats slightly auburn.

The men who worked in the factory smelt of sweat, some of them of wine or garlic, and all of them of something dusty and metallic. Like the smell of the lead in a pencil when it's sharpened. For my work at school I had a pencil sharpener in the form of a globe, it was so small you couldn't tell the countries, only the difference between land and sea.

White the page of the world below. Like the traces of tiny

animals in the snow, the scribbles of what I knew as a child.
Nobody else could read them here. I can see the roof, the
pear tree by the shit-house, the byre we stored wood in with
hives on the balcony—the basin where I washed sheets for
Mother is filled with snow, for there's no trace of it—the
garden beneath the windows, the little orchard, and surrounding all, as a floor surrounds a cat's saucer, the factory grounds.
Every year a man came to the school to explain to us children
why the factory was built where it was and why it was the
pride of the region. Men had come from New York, he said, to
visit it! Then he drew on the blackboard the course of the
river. His was white on black and the one below is black on
white. The river goes through the factory. The factory squats
on the river like a woman peeing. He didn't say that.

Around the beginning of the century, he told the school-
children, men everywhere in the world were dreaming of a
new power which was the power of electricity! This new power
was hidden in our mountains, in their white waterfalls. They
called the waterfalls White Coal! He made it look simple on
the blackboard. Engineers canalised the water in cast-iron
pipes which were two metres in diameter. They let the water,
once captured, fall vertically until it acquired a pressure of
100 kilos per square centimetre, and with this pressure the
water of our waterfalls turned giant wheels in turbines, which,
turning, produced nine million kilowatts of electricity per
hour. The beginning of electro-metallurgy in Europe! he cried.
Vive la République!

Its work done, the river rejoined its course and made its
way to the sea. Do the fish go through the turbines? a child
asked. No, no, dear, answered the man. Why not? We have
filters.

Our house had three rooms. The kitchen where everything
happened and I did my homework. The Pele where my two

brothers slept. And the Third Room where my parents and I slept. In the summer, after we'd brought the hay in, my brothers sometimes liked to sleep in the barn. Then I'd move into the Pele and sleep there alone. Opposite the bed hung a mirror with a black-spotted glass. When I couldn't sleep I lay there and talked to myself. I talked to my little finger. What was in the Beginning? I asked. Silence. Before God created the world and there was no earth, no manganese, and no mountains, what was there? The finger wagged. If you see a spider on a table and you brush him off, the table's still there, if you take the table outside, there's still the floorboards, if you take up the floorboards there's still the earth, if you cart the earth away there's still a sky with stars on the other side of the world, so what was there at the beginning? The finger didn't reply and I bit it.

Seen from the height I'm now at, Father's refusal to sell his farm to the factory looks absurd. We were surrounded. Every year Father was obliged to lead his four cows through an ever larger factory yard over more railway lines. Every year the slag mountains were growing higher, hiding the house and its little plot more effectively from the road and from its own pastures on the other side of the river. The owners first doubled, then trebled, the price they were prepared to pay him. His reply remained the same. My patrimony is not for sale. Later they tried to force him out by law. He said he would dynamite their offices. Now the snow covers all.

My job was to feed the rabbits. In the early spring it was dandelions. Father said there was no other valley in the world with as many dandelions as ours. Dandelion millionaires, he called us. Rabbits eat with such impatience, as if they are eating their way towards life! Their jaws munching the dandelion leaves was the fastest thing I'd ever seen and their muzzles quivered as fast as their jaws munched.

There was a black buck rabbit I hated. He had something evil in his eye. He was always waiting for his evil moment to come and he nipped me with his teeth more than once. Mother stunned the rabbits and strung them up by their hind legs and gouged out their eyes with a knife and they bled to death. When she did this it was always on a Friday, because a rabbit, roasted in the oven with mustard, was a feast to be eaten on Sunday, when the men could stay at the table drinking gnôle after lunch and not go to work.

You can drink two litres of cider and never piss a drop—it all comes out in sweat, Achille my boy, on the furnaces.

I tried to persuade Mother to kill the black rabbit. He's our only big buck, she said. Eventually she cooked him. And to my surprise, I couldn't eat anything. She must be coming down with something, Father said. I couldn't eat because I couldn't stop thinking of how much I hated him.

The moment the snow disappeared, Mother started to nag Father. They're digging their gardens up at Pessy, she'd cry. It's too soon to plant, he'd say, without looking up from his newspaper, the earth's not warm enough. We're always the last! she complained. And our cauliflowers last year? My cauliflowers were as big as buckets, he boasted.

It took Papa three days to turn the earth of the garden and to dig in the manure. I helped him by forking the manure out of the wheelbarrow. The lilac trees were in flower and a cuckoo was singing in the forest above the factory. It was as hot as in June. Father had his shirt-sleeves rolled up, and when he was too hot, he removed his cap and he wiped his bald head, but he refused to take off his black corduroy waistcoat. Every spring he said the same thing: Do the opposite of the walnut tree! I knew the answer to his riddle: the walnut is the first to shed its leaves and the last to come out in leaf.

The garden was almost dug. Its brown earth was raked and

drying in the sun. The first green shoots would soon be appearing in straight rows without a fault, because, just as at school we drew lines in pencil in our exercise books to write our words on, so Mother made a line on the earth with a string when she planted her rows of seed.

My fork had three metal prongs like any other pitchfork, but its wooden shaft was shorter so it was easier for me to handle. Father had made it for me. All the year it leant against the wall by the tap in the stable, ready for when I helped him clean out the stable after the evening milking, my homework done.

Often he complained about my handwriting, and it's true it was not as good as his. He wrote with loops and curlicues as if the whole word were a single piece of string.

The rain does better on the window pane, Odile, write it again!

In the garden he straightened his back, looked at me slyly and said: When you marry, Odile, don't marry a man who drinks.

There isn't a man who doesn't drink! I said.

Fetch me a glass of cider from the cellar, he ordered me, from the barrel on the right.

He drank the cider slowly, looking at the mountains with snow still on them.

I'd give a lot, Odile, to see the man you're going to marry.

You'll see him all right, Papa.

He shook his head and gave me back the glass. No, Odile, I'll never see the man you marry.

He said it smiling, but I couldn't bear him saying it. I couldn't bear the silence of what it meant. I said the first thing that came into my head: I won't marry a man unless I love him, and if I love him, he'll love me, and if we love each other . . . if we love each other, we'll have children, and I'll be too busy to notice if he drinks, Papa, and if he drinks too much too often I'll fetch him cider from the cellar, so many glasses he'll go to sleep in the kitchen and I'll put him to bed as soon as the cows are fed.

The Barracks below are scarcely visible in the snow. I can spot them because of blue smoke coming from a chimney. A woman is crossing the footbridge over the river. The Barracks were three minutes' walk from the factory—the same as our house in the opposite direction. From our house to the footbridge was five minutes' walk. Three if I ran. Mother often sent me to the shop by the Barracks to buy mustard or salt or something she'd forgotten. I walked to the bridge and then ran. At whatever time of day, the men who lived there would cry out and wave. They worked on shifts, and of those not working or sleeping some would be washing their clothes on the grass, some preparing a meal by an open window, some tinkering with an old car they hoped to put on the road. In the winter they lit bonfires outside and they brewed tea and roasted chestnuts. They were forbidden to fish in the river.

If I stopped running they held up their arms and grinned and tried to pat my head. I was always relieved to cross the bridge back to our side. Father said the Company had built the Barracks to house a hundred men as soon as the factory was finished. The Company knew they wouldn't find more than two or three hundred local workers and so they foresaw from the beginning that they would need foreigners. Every man who lodged in the Barracks had his own secrets. Three, four, perhaps more. Impenetrable and unnameable. They turned over these secrets in their hands, wrapped them in paper, threw them in the river, burnt them, whittled them away with their knives when they had nothing else to do. Hundreds of secrets. We in the village on our side of the river had only four. Who killed Lucie Cabrol for her money? Where above Peniel is the entrance to the disused gold mine? What happens at the bridegroom's funeral before they put him in his coffin? Who betrayed the Marmot, who was Michel's uncle, after the factory-gate meeting? Only four secrets. Across the river they in their sheds kept hundreds.

From here, river, house, sheds, factory, bridge, all look like toys. So it was in childhood, Odile Blanc.

One blazing July day in 1950, Mademoiselle Vincent, the schoolmistress, came to the house. I hid in the stable. She wore a hat whose brim was as wide as her shoulders; it was silver-grey in colour and around it was tied a pink satin ribbon.

Merde! said Father. It's the schoolteacher. Look, Louise!

I'll be slipping out, Achille, said Mother.

I have come to talk to you about your daughter, Monsieur Blanc.

Not doing well at school? Do sit down, Mademoiselle Vincent.

On the contrary, I've come to tell you—she scratched her hot freckled shoulder—on the contrary, I've come to tell you how well your Odile is doing.

Kind of you to come all this way to tell us that. A little coffee?

Father poured coffee into a cup, took off his cap and adjusted it further back on his head.

She's never been difficult, has our Odile, he said.

Her intelligence—

I don't know how you see it, Mademoiselle Vincent, but to my way of seeing, intelligence is not—

She is a pupil of great promise.

Wait a year or two, she's only thirteen, said Father. In a year or two her promise—do you take sugar?

It's just because she's thirteen that we have to decide things now, Monsieur Blanc.

Even in my day, Father said, nobody married before sixteen!

I want to propose to you, Monsieur Blanc, that we send Odile to Cluses.

You said she's causing no trouble, Mademoiselle. At least that's what I understood, what sort of trouble?

Mademoiselle Vincent took off her hat and laid it on her lap. Her greying hair, a little damp, was pressed against her scalp.

No trouble, she said slowly, I want her to go to Cluses for her sake.

How for her sake?

If she stays here, Mademoiselle Vincent went on, she'll leave school next year. If she goes to Cluses she can continue until she gets her CAP. Let her go to Cluses. She was fanning herself with a little notebook taken from her handbag.

She'd have to be a boarder? asked Father.

Yes.

Have you mentioned it to her?

Not before talking to you, Monsieur Blanc.

He shrugged his shoulders, looked at the barometer, said nothing.

Mademoiselle Vincent got to her feet, holding her hat.

I knew you'd see reason, she said, offering him her hand like a present.

I was watching through the stable door.

Nothing to do with reason! shouted Father. In God's name! Nothing to do with reason. He paused, gave a little laugh, and leered at Mademoiselle Vincent. She was an old man's last sin—I wonder if you can understand that, Mademoiselle—his last sin.

It will mean a lot of work, she said.

Don't push her too hard, said Father, it won't change anything. You'll see I was right one day. Odile will be married before she's eighteen. At seventeen she'll be married.

We can't know, Monsieur Blanc. I hope she goes on to take her Baccalaureate.

Back of my arse! You see Odile as a schoolteacher?

She might be, said Mademoiselle Vincent.

No, no. She's too untidy. To be a teacher you have to be very tidy.

I'm not very tidy, said Mademoiselle Vincent, take me, I'm not very tidy.

You have a fine voice, Mademoiselle, when you sing, you make people happy. That makes up for a lot.

You're a flatterer, Monsieur Blanc.

She'll never be a teacher, Odile, she's too . . . he hesitated. She's too—too close to the ground.

Funny to think of those words now in the sky.

Twice in my life I've been homesick and both times it was in Cluses. The first time was the worst, for then I hadn't yet lived anything worse than homesickness. It's to do with life, homesickness, not death. In Cluses the first time I didn't yet know this difference.

The school was a building of five storeys. I wasn't used to staircases. I missed the smell of the cows, Papa raking out the fire, Maman emptying her piss-pot, everyone in the family doing something different and everybody knowing where everybody else was, Emile playing with the radio and my screaming at him, I missed the wardrobe with my dresses all mixed up with Maman's, and the goat tapping with her horns against the door.

Ever since I could remember, everyone had always known who I was. They called me Odile or Blanc's Daughter or Achille's Last. If somebody did not know who I was, a single answer to a single question was enough for them to place me. Ah yes! Then you must be Régis's sister! In Cluses I was a stranger to everyone. My name was Blanc, which began with a B, and so I was near the top of the alphabetical list. I was always among the first ten that had to stand up, or to file out.

In the school there I learnt how to look at words like something written on a blackboard. When a man swears, the words come out of his body like shit. As kids we talked like that all the time—except when we made traps with words. Adam and Eve and Pinchme went down to the river to bathe, Adam and Eve were drowned, who do you think was saved? At Cluses I learnt that words belonged to writing. We used them; yet they were never entirely ours.

One evening after the last lesson I went back into the classroom to fetch a book I'd forgotten. The French mistress was sitting at her table, her head buried in her hands, and she was crying. I didn't dare approach her. On the blackboard behind her, I remember it so well, was the conjugation of the verb *fuir*.

If somebody had asked me in 1952: What place makes you think of men most? I wouldn't have said the factory, I wouldn't have said the café opposite the church when there was a funeral, I wouldn't have said the autumn cattle market, I'd have said: the edge of a wood! Take all the edges of all the forests and copses in the valley and put them end to end like a screen, and there'd be a frieze of men! Some with guns, some with dogs, others with chain saws, a few with girls. I heard their voices from the road below. I looked at them, the slimness of the young ones, the way their checkered shirts hung loose, their boots, the way they wore their trousers, the bulges just below where their belts were fastened. I didn't notice their faces, I didn't bother to name them. If one of them noticed me, I'd be off. I didn't want to say a word and I didn't want to approach them. Watching was quite enough, and watching them, I knew how the world was made.

Take this loaf to Régis, said Mother. When it's freezing

so hard the cold penetrates to your very bones and a man needs his food in such weather.

She handed me the bread. I ran as fast as I could towards the factory; there was ice everywhere and I had to pick my way. All was frozen—railway points, locks, window frames, ruts, the cliff face behind the factory was hung with icicles, only the river still moved. At the entrance I called to the first man I could see, he had bloodshot eyes and spoke with a strong Spanish accent.

Régis! Big man of honour! he shouted and jerked his thumb upwards. I waited there on the threshold for several minutes, stamping my feet to keep them warm. When Régis arrived he was with Michel. They were of the same class: '51. They had done their military service together.

You know Michel? asked Régis.

I knew Michel. Michel Labourier, nephew of the Marmot.

For God's sake come in and get warm, hissed Régis between his teeth as I handed him the loaf.

Father—

It's not the same if you're with me. Give me your hand. Jesus! you're cold! We've just tapped her.

They led me away from the big furnaces and the massive cranes overhead, which moved on rails in heaven, to another much smaller workshop.

You're going to school at Cluses? Michel asked me.

I nodded.

Do you like it?

I miss being at home.

At least you'll learn something there.

It's another world, I said.

Nonsense! It's the same bloody world. The difference is the kids who go to Cluses don't stay poor and dumb.

We're not dumb, I said.

He looked at me hard. Here, he said, take this to keep your brains warm. He gave me his woolen cap, red and black. I protested and he pulled the cap down on my head, laughing.

He's a communist, said Régis later.

At that time I didn't know what the word meant. We sat against a wall on a pile of sand. I let a handful of it run through my frozen fingers. I could feel its warmth through my stockings, touching my calves. Régis rummaged in a tin, took out his knife, and began cutting a sausage. There were some other men at the end of the shop.

So here's your sister come to see us! shouted one of them.

Odile's her name.

There's a Saint Odile, did you know that?

Yes, I shouted, her fête is the thirteenth of December.

She was born blind in Alsace, the man shouted back. He was at least fifty and thin as a goat's leg.

Was she?

She saw with her eyes for the first time when she was grown up. Then she founded a monastery.

The thin old man, who wasn't from the valley and who knew all about Saint Odile, was pulling on the chains of a pulley which worked a machine for grasping and lifting massive weights.

Now he's going to take the hat off the bread, said Régis.

I've just given you the bread, I said, understanding nothing.

See over there what's sizzling?

In the sand?

That's the bread with its hat on. Now watch!

Several men began to prod at the bread with long bars. To every blow the thing responded by spitting out fire. I was eating sausage. The old man's machine came down and lifted the top off the bread as if it were a cap. Under the cap everything was incandescent. I could feel the onrush of heat, although I was at the other end of the shop. The edges of the white-hot underneath were dribbling like a ripe cheese. When a dribble fell off and hit the ground it made a brittle noise like glass and turned black. All the men were holding up shields in front of their faces.

Each bread weighs a ton, said Régis. He drank from a bottle of wine and some of the wine ran down his neck. A ton, he continued, and ferromolybdenum is worth six thousand a kilo—work it out for yourself, you're still in school—one bread is sold for how much?

Six million.

Correct.

The bread, one and a half metres in diameter, was now phosphorescent in the sand. Régis wasn't looking any longer. I couldn't take my eyes off it.

Do you know the story of the Two Hunters? Régis asked.

Which story?

The story of the Two Hunters in the Forest.

The bread was changing colour. Its whiteness was turning violet. The violet of a child with croup.

I don't think I know the story of the Two Hunters.

Once there were two hunters in the forest up at Peniel: Jean-Paul and Jean-Marc.

Water from a pipe in the roof, with hundreds of holes in it, was falling like rain onto the bread. It was scarlet now.

Jean-Paul stops and says: Look over there, Jean-Marc! I can't see anything, replies Jean-Marc. Jean-Paul, still pointing, says: You must be blind, over there by the spruce, the one that's been uprooted. I can see the root and the earth and the stones, Jean-Paul, I can't see more.

The rain falling on the bread was making steam and it was hissing like a cricket.

The two hunters go deeper into the forest. Can you see

her now? shouts Jean-Paul. Where? By the snow under the roots, Jean-Marc. In God's name, yes! screams Jean-Marc. Both men stop in their tracks, then they start making their way towards the tree. The snow is up to their waists. After a while they stop to get their breath back.

The bread was getting darker and darker in colour and I could scarcely see it anymore because of the clouds of steam coming off it.

Alive? asks Jean-Marc. Jean-Paul pushes his way forward. I can feel it from here! he cries. Be careful, Jean-Paul! Careful, Jean-Paul! Jean-Paul disappears. After a moment Jean-Marc hears his friend laughing, then his laugh changes into a sigh. The happiest sigh in the world, my friend. Jean-Marc knows what is happening so he looks at the tree tops. Whilst he looks at the tree tops, he counts. When he's counted to five thousand, he looks down, towards the spruce. No sign of Jean-Paul. Now it's Jean-Marc's turn.

The rain on the bread had stopped.

Jean-Marc too can feel it. He can hear the dripping. Like Jean-Paul, he falls forward onto his face and starts to laugh. His laugh too becomes a sigh.

The bread was black now, with colours in it like oil.

Do you know what they were doing, Jean-Paul and Jean-Marc?

I shook my head.

You don't know, Odile, what the two hunters were doing? No.

They were doing the lying-down waltz!

I looked at Régis and I thought: My kid brother—he was nine years older than I—you're drinking too much.

The sheet sail and everything hanging from it is turning south, towards the sun in a sky of the deepest winter blue, like the blue we had to wash clothes with.

On the day when Christ ascended to heaven, the Brass Band went from hamlet to hamlet in the village playing music. Their uniforms were newly pressed, their instruments were glittering in the sun, and the leaves of the beech trees were fresh as lettuces. They played so loud they made the windows rattle and tiles fall off the roof. And after each concert in each hamlet the public offered them gnôle and cakes, so that by the end of the afternoon on Ascension Day, after a number of little concerts, the first and second saxophones were drunk as well as several trombones and a drum or two. On Ascension night, Father came home with his trumpet a little bit the worse for wear. With Father, though, nobody could tell till the evening. He never let it influence his fingers when playing.

He died on February the ninth, 1953. The next Ascension Day the band came to play in our orchard in his honour. They played a march from Verdi's *Aïda* and a tune called "Amazing Grace." Men from the factory lined the fence of the orchard listening to the music. Mother stood by the stable doors, arms folded across her bosom, looking up at the sky. And suddenly Papa's house with its three rooms, its hayloft, its little wooden balcony, its chopped wood, dwarfed the factory which was the size of six cathedrals.

"Amazing Grace" begins sad and gradually the sadness becomes a chorus and so is no longer sad but defiant. For a while I believed he was there. Later the music listens to itself and discovers that something has fallen silent. Irretrievably. He had left.

Whilst I was listening to "Amazing Grace" on that afternoon in May 1953, I touched something which I wouldn't be able to name until twenty years later. I touched the truth that the virility which women look for in men is often sly, slippery, impudent. It's not grand, what they're looking for. It's cautious and cunning, just like Father was.

The men on the other side of the fence started to clap and Michel waved at me. I turned away, saying to myself that only a communist would wave at a moment like that!

Michel's motorbike was red and was made in Czechoslovakia. The spare parts for it were cheaper than for any other bike, Michel said, because Czechoslovakia was communist and the communists didn't put profit before everything else. On several Sundays he asked me if I'd like to go for a spin with him and each time I refused. He was too sure of himself, he thought he knew better than anybody else in the valley. He had called my Father a Chopping Block. Not to me. I heard about it from a friend. Achille Blanc has been a chopping block for others all his life! Those were his words. So I said no to him.

The sixth time he asked me was in August. We were both on holiday. The hay was in the barn. Régis had bought an old third-hand Peugeot and was painting it in the orchard. Emile was there in the house when Michel came. He drives well, Odile, said Emile, you've nothing to be frightened about. On Wednesday morning early, Michel announced, I'll pick you up at five. At five! I protested. Five's not too early if we're going to Italy! Italy! I screamed. Yet, however loud I screamed it, the word was having its effect. If we were really going to drive to Italy, everything was beyond my control. I said nothing more. And on Tuesday night I prepared my trousers, my boots, and a haversack with a picnic for us both.

We went over the Grand St. Bernard a little to the east of the Mont Blanc where the wind now is blowing the snow like my chiffon scarf against the blue sky. Neither of us knew what life had in store. Nothing happened. Michel had brought a thermos of coffee which we drank from for the first time near Chamonix. We passed a factory which, Michel said, was like a copy of ours. It took up less space. On the bike we

climbed higher and higher. We ate our picnic above the tree
line. I never breathed so much air in my life. Mouth, nose,
ears and eyes all took in air. At the summit we threw snowballs
at each other and saw the dogs. They were as big as ponies.
There was a lake. A lake at that height was as surprising as
tears at a victory. When the wind was too cold I put my head
down against his leather jacket. I tucked my knees under his
legs and held on with one hand to his leather belt. Around
the hairpins I lay down with the bike like grass blown by
the wind.

She overheated a bit on the last stretch, he said. You probably smelt the burnt oil?

Motor oil, I said, I don't know what it smells like.

On the red 350cc two-stroke twin motor bike made in
Czechoslovakia we came down into Italy, on the other side
of the mountain. The cows looked poorer, the goats thinner,
there was less wood and more rocks, yet the air was like a kiss.
In such air women didn't have to be like we were on our side
of the mountain. Where we have wild raspberries in ruined
pine forests, I told myself, they have grapes on vines which
grow between apple trees! For the first time in my life I was
envious.

Did you notice the Saumua coming down to Aosta? he
asked.

No.

It's the biggest truck since the war. Takes a load of thirty
tons.

We arrived back before it was dark. I was in time to shut
up the chickens and take the milk on my back to the dairy.
My behind was sore, my hands were grimy, my hair was
tangled. It took me hours to untangle it before I went to sleep.
But I was proud of myself. I'd been to Italy.

We'll do another trip, Michel proposed.

School begins next week.

You're a funny one, Odile, there's no school on Sunday.

No, I said, thanks for this time.

You're a good passenger, I'll say that for you.

Are there bad ones?

Plenty. They don't trust the driver astride the machine. You can't ride a bike if you don't let go. I'm willing to bet you weren't frightened for a moment, Odile. You had confidence, didn't you? You weren't frightened for a moment, were you?

Maybe yes and maybe no. His sureness made me want to tease him.

A weekend, two months later, I was coming home from Cluses and the bus driver said:

Have you heard what happened to Michel?

Michel who?

Michel Labourier. You didn't hear about his accident?

On his motorbike?

No, in the factory.

What happened?

Lost both his legs.

Where is he?

Lyons. It's the best hospital in the country for burns. A military hospital. They used to fight wars with lead, now they fight them with flames. Both legs gone.

I stared through the bus window and I saw nothing, not even the factory when we passed it. The next day I went to see his mother.

Perhaps it would have been better, she said, if it had killed him outright.

No, I said, no, Madame Labourier.

He's not allowed visitors, she said, he's in a glass cage.

I'm sure you'll be able to visit him soon.

It's too far. Too far for anyone to go.

Is he still in danger?

For his life, no.

Don't cry, Madame Labourier, don't cry.

I cried when I thought about it every evening for a week in Cluses. For a man to lose both legs. I thought too about what the boys call their third leg. When you're young and both your legs are supple your third leg goes stiff . . . when you're old and your legs are stiff, your third leg goes limp. And this silly joke made me cry more.

New Year's Eve, 1953, I spent at home. Father's chair was empty. After supper Régis and Emile got up to go to the dance in the village. Come on, Odile, said Emile. I'll stay with Mother. You like dancing! insisted Emile. There's no boy in the village good enough for our Odile now, said Régis. They left. Mother sewed and went to bed early. I heard the bells pealing at midnight on the radio and the crowds cheering. I wasn't sleepy and so I let myself out and walked once round the orchard. The grass was as hard as iron. The bise had been blowing for several days and the sky was clear. Looking up at the stars, I thought of Father. Nobody can look up at the stars when they are so hard and bright and not think that they don't have something to say. Then I thought of Michel without his legs and the Red Star he wore on his leather jacket. In their silence I missed his jokes and his cough. I went to check that the chicken house was well shut. When it was minus fifteen for a week on end, the foxes would cross the factory yard looking for food. A month earlier the night shift had killed a wild boar behind the turbine house. Suddenly the wind changed and to my amazement I heard dance music. A tune from a band wafting towards me. It seemed to come in waves, just as the stars seemed to twinkle. Distance and cold can do strange things. I made up my mind. I returned to

the house, put my hair in a scarf, and found an old army coat.
I would go and see what was happening at the Ram's Run.

Every New Year's Eve the Company imported a band to the
factory and the men who were lodged in the Barracks had
their own dance. The villagers didn't participate, the Company
didn't encourage them to, and it was for this reason that it
was called the Ram's Run. I crossed the railway line. The
music was louder. The furnaces were throbbing as usual. The
smoke from the chimney stacks was white in the starlight.
Otherwise everything was still and frozen. Not a soul to be
seen outside. The ground-floor rooms adjoining the office
block were lit up. There were no curtains and the windows
were misted over.

I crept up to one and scraped like a mouse with my finger-
nail. I couldn't believe my eyes, there was a man who was
dancing sitting down on the floor! He had his hands on his
hips and he threw out his feet in front of him and his feet
came back as fast as they went out, like balls bouncing off a
wall. I was so amazed I didn't notice the approach of the
stranger who was now at my side looking down at me.

Good evening, he said. Why don't you come into the warm?

I shook my head.

You must be hot-blooded, not to mind the cold on a night
like this!

It's only minus fifteen, I said.

Those were the first words I spoke to him. After them there
was a silence. The two of us stood there by the light of the
window, our breaths steamy and entwining like puffs from
the nostrils of the same horse.

What's your name?

Odile.

Your name in full?

Mademoiselle Odile Blanc.

He stood to attention like a soldier and bowed his head. He must have been two metres tall. His hair was cropped short and he had enormous thumbs, his hands pressed against his thighs, his thumbs were as big as sparrows.

My name is Stepan Pirogov.

Where were you born?

Far away.

In a valley?

Somewhere which is flat, flat, flat.

No rivers?

There's a river there called the Pripiat.

Ours is called the Giffre.

Blanc? Blanc means white like milk?

Not always—not when you order vin blanc!

White like snow, no?

Not the white of an egg! I shouted.

Give me one more joke, he said and opened the door.

I was standing in the vestibule of the Ram's ballroom. After the glacial air outside, it felt very warm. There was the noise of men talking—like the sound of the fermentation of fruit in a barrel. There was a strong smell of sour wine, scent, and the red dust that in the end powders every ledge and every flat surface facing upwards in the factory. Along one wall of the vestibule—which was really an anteroom to the offices, where the clerical staff took off their coats and put on their aprons—there was a long table where women whom I'd never seen before were serving drinks to a group of men who had obviously been drinking for a longer time than was good for them. My brother said that the women for the Ram's Run were hired by the company and brought from far away, somewhere near Lyons, in a bus.

I wanted to get out into the air and I wanted him not to forget me immediately. So I told him a story about my grand-

mother. It wasn't strictly my grandmother. It was the woman
my grandfather lived with after his wife was dead. When he
died, Céline—she was called Céline—continued to live in
grandfather's house alone. She was old by then. You can't
explain all that to a stranger whom you've just met a few
minutes before and who has taken you into a bar full of men
with the windows steamed up and the floorboards muddy and
wet with melted ice. So I told him it was my grandmother.

Grandma always had a billygoat, so the neighbours had the
habit of bringing their goats to her when they were in heat.
She used to charge a thousand a visit, and if the goat didn't
take they had another visit for nothing. One year, every single
neighbour who had come with a goat in heat demanded a
second visit. Something was wrong. Grandmother talked
about it to Nestor the gravedigger who was married to her
niece and bred rabbits whose skins were sold as otter. It's
simple, he said to her, he's too cold, in your stable all alone,
the he-goat must be freezing. Build him a stall where he'll
keep warm! Grandma went home and thought about Nestor's
advice and decided it was too much trouble. Instead, she'd
bring the beast into the kitchen—except when the sun was out.
The he-goat recovered and all the neighbours' goats were going
to have kids at Eastertime. When Grandma next saw Nestor
the gravedigger, she thanked him for his advice. So you built
him a stall? he said. Too much trouble, she replied, I brought
him into the kitchen. Nestor looked surprised. And the smell?
he asked. Grandma shrugged her shoulders. What do you
expect with a he-goat, she said, he soon got used to it!

I was glad when he laughed. Then I caught sight of myself
in a mirror above a sink. What was I doing here? Quickly I
turned away from the mirror. He stood there, towering above
me, protective like a tree. And hesitating. Perhaps under the
neon light I was a surprise to him. Perhaps outside he had

thought I was older. Perhaps he hadn't seen how ridiculous my clothes were. Despite myself I glanced at the mirror again.

Your feet must be cold, he said.

I looked down at my thick, artificial-fur-lined boots and shook my head.

If we dance, they'll warm up! And at that moment the band, whom I couldn't see, started to play. A polka. This man, to whom I'd told the story about the goat, took my arm and delicately guided me towards the Ram's Run. The band were installed on planks laid on scaffolding. All the other women wore high-heeled shoes. The music sounded strange, for the room, which was normally a storeroom, had no ceiling. Far up, high above were the iron girders of the same roof which covered the topmost furnace. Most of the women were wearing low-cut dresses and some wore golden bracelets. There were also men dancing with each other. And one woman dancing alone with a gigantic feather.

What's so surprising about music is that it comes from the outside. It feels as if it comes from the inside. The man who had clicked his heels and announced his name as Stepan Pirogov was dancing with Odile Blanc. Yet inside the music, which was inside me, Odile and Stepan were the same thing. If he had touched me whilst we were dancing like men touch women, I'd have slapped his face. Behind the band there was a heap of shovels, if he had touched me, I would have taken a shovel to him. He knew better. He didn't interfere with what the music was doing. He tossed back his head at each beat, chin flung up, neck taut, mouth smiling. When the band stopped, he lifted his hand off my shoulder and stared at the players as if surprised that there was no more music, then he nodded and the band started up again. It looked as though he ordered the music with a nod of his head.

For a long while, I don't know how long, before we had

exchanged anything except a silly story about a goat, before anything had been decided between us, when I knew nothing of Stepan Pirogov, the two of us let the music fill us like a single cart drawn uphill by a cantering horse.

Are you thirsty? he eventually asked.

We returned to the vestibule with its neon lights, where he bought me a lemonade. This time I avoided looking in the mirror. His accent was very foreign.

Where is it you live, Odile?

In the house after the shunting line stops.

Where the cows are? My father kept a cow.

Just one?

Just one, outside Stockholm.

Were you born in Stockholm?

I don't know where I was born.

Your mother could tell you.

I never knew my mother.

She's dead?

No.

In the heat and the smell of sour wine and the din of the men's laughter in the Ram's Run, I suddenly felt a kind of pity for him. Or was it a pity for both of us? I gazed at the lemonade in the bottom of my glass. I could feel him looking down at me—like a tree at a rabbit. I raised my head. My sudden fear had gone.

I've been here three months, he said.

And before?

Before I was on a ship.

A sailor?

If you like.

You won't stay here long if you're a sailor!

I'd stay long for you, he said.

You know nothing about me!

I've known you since I was first conceived in the womb of a mother I never knew. He pronounced this extraordinary sentence in a strange singsong voice.

I have to go, I said.

Spend a little more of the year with me, Odile.

Is that how you talk in your language? I asked.

In my language I'd call you Dilenka.

It was different dancing with him the second time. I'm dancing with a sailor, I kept telling myself. If mother knew I was dancing with a sailor.

I've never seen the sea in my life. When the dance was over, I went to fetch my coat.

I have to work tomorrow, I told him.

Can I see you on Saturday afternoon?

I may have to work, I don't know.

I'll be waiting for you by the footbridge, he said.

What time? I could have bitten off my tongue for saying that.

I'll be there the whole afternoon, listening to the river till you come. He said this in the same singsong voice.

My mother was washing out a bucket in the stable and I was milking before taking the bus to Cluses, it was still dark—and she screamed at me:

You would never have dared do that, if your father was still alive!

Do what?

Go to the Ram's Run!

There was no harm in it, Mother.

And to come back at four in the morning!

Three!

No one goes to the Ram's Run!

They're not beasts.

What did I do—what in God's name did I do—to deserve a daughter like you?

You did with Papa—may he rest in peace—what most wives do, Mother.

Listen to her! my mother was screaming. She talks like that to her own mother.

She hurled the bucketful of water at me. It was so cold it took my breath away and the shock of it made me fall off the stool. Lilac calmly turned her head to see what had happened. Cows are the calmest cows in the world, was one of Stepan's jokes. He would say it in a mournful voice.

I kept him waiting the whole afternoon by the footbridge. When at last I arrived, he didn't complain. He stood there listening and whilst I talked, he fingered the fringe of the scarf I had round my neck. It was so cold, the sound of the river was as shrill as the train's whistle. A train came once a fortnight to take away the molybdenum and manganese. Always at night. And since my earliest childhood the train woke me up. We walked across the lines to the big furnace shop.

Do you know each furnace has a name? he asked. The big one there is called Peter. The other one is called Tito . . . Why does it make you smile?

They weren't called those names when I was young.

Now he was smiling.

There's another called Napoleon. Why does it make you smile?

A little smile, I said.

Not so little now! he said.

Smaller than yours!

Do you know how to measure a smile?

Yes, I said.

He bent down and picked me up so my mouth was level with his, and he kissed me. On the nose.

I know so little about him, yet with the years of thinking I have learnt a great deal more from the same few facts. Perhaps there are never many facts when you first love somebody.

The facts are what destiny has in store for you. His foster parents were Ukrainians and left Russia in the early twenties to settle in Sweden. One day a Russian who knew his foster mother when she was in Kiev arrived with a swaddled bundle. In it was a two-month-old baby. The couple gave the baby their family name of Pirogov. They had no children of their own. The "father" was a chairmaker and the "mother" took in washing. They had had to leave their country because in 1918 the man had joined the wrong army—the green not the red one. His "father" joined the army of a man whom Stepan called Batko Makhno. Batko, he said, meant Father. I didn't understand much.

The winter passed slowly. One Saturday we went for a walk in the snow. He was wearing blue wool mittens. As we walked, his arm round my neck and one of his huge blue woolen hands on my shoulder, he told me a story.

Once there were two bears asleep under a rock. Their fur was all white with hoarfrost. The smaller of the two opened her eyes.

Mischka! she growled.

Mouchenka! growled the other.

We can speak! Say something. Say a word.

Honey, he growled.

Snow, she said.

Spring, he said.

Death, she said.

Why death? asked Mischka.

As soon as we speak, we know death.

God! said Mischka and pushed his muzzle into her neck.

Why does God have so little power? asked Mouchenka, and placed a paw on his back.

How should I know?

Everything that exists hides him, she said.

He's in his lair, he said.

He could come out, couldn't he? complained Mouchenka.

Mouchenka moved her head from the shelter of the rock and the snow fell on her large black muzzle. Mischka, why does he have so little power?

Because he created the world, growled the bear.

So he spent all his power doing that and has been exhausted ever since! She blew the snow off her mouth.

No, said Mischka.

What do you mean, No?

He could have created everything differently so it did exactly what he wanted.

That would have been better?

Yes.

For a long while the two bears said nothing. At last the she-bear said: If it did exactly what he wanted, no one would recognise him! Don't you see? There'd be no need to recognise him. There'd be nothing else but him!

Mouchenka! You were simpler when you couldn't speak.

As things are, she went on, he hopes to be recognised all the while. Keeps sending reminders. Look at the snow falling, Mischka, it's falling on every pine needle.

He's clever, growled the he-bear, he's made it all so he stays hidden! He scratched the fur on her hip with his paw. He's made it all so he can be left in peace!

No, no, said Mouchenka, God made the world as it is, so he should be needed. It's what he wanted.

At that very moment two shots rang out, and a hunter shouted: Bagged the two of them!

The blood of the two bears stained first their fur and later the snow.

Christian is pointing at something below. He is wearing the woolen gloves which I knitted for him. I can't make out what he's pointing at.

The next weekend I suggested Stepan should come to the

house. I told him about my brothers. I was hoping that if Mother saw him she might relent a little. Since the morning when she had thrown the water in the stable, she hadn't addressed a single word to me.

Not yet, Dilenka, not yet. You take a man home for the first time and everyone looks at him and starts wondering about the future, they try him on—like a pair of trousers—to see how he fits. If I were your age, but I'm a fully grown man, a foreigner, I don't have anything here, and they'll need a lot of reassuring—it's too soon, I don't know yet where to take you. Let's wait a little.

One Saturday Stepan came to Cluses by the midday bus. He wanted to see the room in the widow Besson's house, where I lodged. This time it was I who was against the visit. The room was too small and the bed took up half the space. Instead, I had a present for him. I'd wrapped it up in a scarf of mine, a white chiffon scarf.

What can it be? he asked.

It was a hip flask for gnôle with leather round it. I saved up for a month to buy it. Stepan had complained about the cold when he was working on night shift.

Charge Peter with shovels, six tons, *schest!* Stay near and his heat dries up the sweat so it burns you. Step back and you freeze in the night air. Minus twenty-eight. *Minus dvadtzat vossiem.*

He taught me to count in Russian, and I learnt like boys learn to imitate birds.

May a mouthful of gnôle on your night shift keep you company between the hot and the cold! I wrote that sentence on an envelope and I stuck the envelope to the flask before I gave it to him.

When he read the message on the envelope, he threw the flask up in the air and caught it in one hand. We were stand-

ing in front of the bus station in Cluses. Then he kissed me.
On the mouth. Each time it was for longer.

Father's friend, César the water-diviner, used to hold a
pendulum over a local map and wherever there was buried
water in the earth, it began to turn in circles like a duckling.
Am I circling over the Mole because on a Sunday in May
Stepan and I climbed there to pick globeflowers? A woman I
could shout to on the path below is wearing a dress I never had.
How much we will be forgotten!

Whilst we climbed, Stepan told me about his childhood. I
was brought up, he said, to the smell of fish glue—the smell
of the ocean bed. And I don't know if you'll believe me but
it's true: I could hold nails between my teeth as soon as I was
eating solid food. I made my first chair when I was fifteen,
and Father maintained—like a true disciple of Makhno—he
maintained it was better than any throne in the world!

The sun was hot and it was the time of May when the grass
goes mad with growth. As a child I believed I could see it
growing. The tin roofs of the chalets when we reached the
alpage were crackling in the heat. Stepan didn't know where
the noise came from. Somebody's throwing stones! he said.
There was nobody. Just the two of us.

My father and I disagreed about one thing, he went on,
only one thing and what a thing! Stepan had never seen globeflowers before. I picked some for him. They're like brass
buttons, he said, who cleans them? I laughed. We disagreed
about one thing, he went on. I thought of Russia as my country and I wanted to go back and my father, who was really
my stepfather, was against it. When I was eighteen, after the
victory over the Germans, I filled in the forms for repatriation. Repatriation! he screamed at me in Russian. You weren't
even born there! You don't know anything! You have to be
Russian to be so stupid!

Stepan held five golden flowers to my shoulder and said in his singsong voice: Five Stars! The rest is ashes. You're a General. Generalissimo Odile Achilovich!

Did you get your passport? I asked him.

No, they refused me. No homeland.

I put our bunch of flowers in a little spring so they could drink, and we lay on our backs looking up at the sky, just as now I'm on my stomach looking down on the earth. Stepan put his hand on me and started to caress me. Today I won't stop him, I said to myself. He was talking about cities, asking me to which one I'd like to go to—to London, to Milan, to Rotterdam, to Oslo, to Glasgow? It had never occurred to me before that somebody could choose where to live. It seemed unnatural. No, said Stepan, it's simple with these—he held up both huge hands over my face—I can work anywhere in the world. Where, where will we go, Odile? Instead of answering him, I scrambled to my feet and ran like a wild thing down the hill towards the pine trees. When he came after me I shouted at him: You're a Bohemian! A Bohemian, that's what you are. I never want to see you again! I left him at the bus station. I wouldn't let him walk me to the widow Besson's house. I gave her the flowers and the old lady thanked me and touched my forehead. Haven't you a little fever? You look all flushed. I shook my head to hide my tears from her. Go to bed, Odile, and I'll make you some verveine tea, she said. Perhaps you had too much sun.

After the day of the globeflowers, Stepan posted me a letter. It was the only piece of writing I ever saw by him. I will look to see whether it's still in the tilleul tin. He had written everything in capitals, as children do when they are first learning. The letter said: We need go nowhere, we'll stay here, I'm arranging it, will be waiting for you by the bridge, Saturday. Mischka. I never heard him before or afterwards refer to himself as Mischka.

I was able to get home on that Friday night. Mother was still not talking to me. Emile grinned as he always grinned, and after the soup conspiratorially offered me one of his cigarettes. I was still smoking it when Régis came in. It was several weeks since I'd seen Régis. He was furious. It's got to stop, Odile, do you hear me? He was shouting very loud. It can't go on, do you hear me? You've got to put an end to it, do you hear me? If Father was alive, he'd have stopped you long ago, and you would have obeyed him, do you hear me? Father wouldn't have shouted like you do, I said, and he wouldn't have thought like you and Mother do. Don't be stupid, Sister. Jesus, don't be stupid! Father knew I'd be married by the age of seventeen. There was a silence. Emile was cleaning his nails with a pocketknife. Do you realise that your dolt from Sweden is married? It's a lie, you've made it up! What do you expect, Odile, he's nearly thirty. You don't know anything about him! We've often worked on the same shift, we call him the Snow Shovel, he's crap. Why do you say he's married? Listen, Sister, to what I have to say, married or unmarried, if you persist in going out with that shit we plan to give him a lesson. Back to your field, Swede. He's Russian! All the better, back behind his Iron Curtain!

Was he a married man? The priest later asked me when I confessed, and I had to confess further that I didn't know, and that I'd never asked him. I went to meet him by the footbridge the day after the evening of Régis's threats. I told him nothing because as soon as Stepan was there, palpable, before my eyes, I realised that, should it come to a fight, Régis didn't stand a chance.

We crossed the river, left the Barracks behind us, and climbed to the forest. There we walked along its edge until the factory and the house were out of sight. By the old chapel with its broken windows and the wall behind its altar pocked with bullet marks, we turned in and crossed the forest to come out on the path that leads to Le Mont. There we owned a small barn for storing hay. Now it is in ruins. I'd been there as a child with my father in the days when he brought down hay on a sledge. In my pocket I had the key.

I'd never before seen a man naked like Stepan. I'd seen my father and my brothers at the sink washing all over, I'd seen everything, but I'd never seen a man naked like that. The sight of him brought back to me the night I'd first met him in the Ram's Run, for I was filled with the same kind of pity—was it a pity for both of us?—and this pity was mixed with fear. Yet it wasn't with fear that my heart was pounding. My heart was pounding with excitement at the news it received: its life would never be the same again, the body it pumped for would never be the same again.

Father was an expert grafter of fruit trees. He scarcely ever failed. Onto our wild apple trees he grafted pippins and russets, onto the wild pears, dolbos and williams. He knew at exactly which moment to graft, where to cut, how to bandage. It was as if the sap were in his thumbs. He's grafting me! I said to myself with my arms round Stepan's body. Along the new branches fruit will come like we've never known, neither he nor me. It wasn't easy for Stepan. I wasn't easy to break through. For a moment he was discouraged. I could feel it. Everything about men is so obvious that even I, at seventeen, could understand. And I shared his impatience, that's what I shared with him. So I helped him, like I used to help Father when he was grafting. I'd hold the shoot at the angle needed—whilst Father bound with the cord.

The sunlight streamed through the knotholes of the wall planks and the hay smelt like burnt milk and I felt that everything good that could ever happen was being grafted into me. And next week, we were eating the fruit, weren't we? If only you could have taken more! He gave us very little, dear God.

Yet perhaps not. Sometimes when I tell myself the story of the two bears I say: perhaps the one thing He doesn't understand is time! How long did we lie behind the grey wood with the sunbeams? You never seemed so small as then, Stepanuschka. I was going to be your wife and the mother of your children, and the ocean which I'll never see of your ferry boat. The days were nearly at their longest. When we left, it was dark and there was a moon, we could see the path. On the way down I undid your belt. What I saw, dear God, is where? Where?

They started to build. I don't know with what words Stepan persuaded or inspired them. They started to build a room. Each shed of the Barracks was designated with a letter. I think that when they were first built the letters of the sheds went regularly from A to H. Then some man lodging there had an idea to make a joke which consisted of changing the letters. From the time I could first read as a child the eight sheds were marked IN EUROPA. I could see where the original letters had been painted over. As for the joke, the man who thought it funny had long since left and nobody now could ask him to explain. The letters remained as he had painted them. The N of the IN was written the wrong way round, И. The Company scarcely ever intruded into the Barracks area. There was only one law in the factory that counted: that the ten furnaces be tapped the required number of times every twenty-four hours, and that the castings conform to standard when chemically analysed.

Stepan lived in shed A, which was the last one, on the edge of the factory grounds. Beyond was a plantation of pine trees. The men in shed A were building a room for Stepan. It took them a week of their free time. A partition of planks, a hole in the roof for a chimney and a new door. This room was to be separate from the rest of the dormitory, it was to be private.

Stepan was making a bed, a large bed with a headboard made of oak and a carved rose at each corner. It was the first bed he'd made and it took much more time than the room. You want us to be married? he asked me. I would like to be your wife. I will marry you, he said, it's a promise.

Shed A is still there, the furthest from the bridge. People said he took advantage of me. They knew nothing, those people. They didn't see him carving the roses. If he didn't marry me immediately it was because he couldn't—perhaps because his papers weren't in order. Because he was already married, people said. Perhaps, long before, he did have another wife in another country, in another century. All I know is that he didn't deceive me.

One day you and I, when our grandchildren are off our hands, one day, he said, you and I will go and visit the Ukraine.

From the window of the little makeshift room at the end of shed A, I watched the swallows flying between the Barracks and the lines of spruce. It was ridiculous now for a woman living my life to still be at school, and so I left without taking any exams. As I walked away from the school for the last time through the tall wrought-iron gates, made for horsemen carrying flags, I felt Father very close. It was as if he came with me to ask for a job at the Components Factory, it was as if because of his presence they gave me a job straightaway.

My first was pressing holes in a tiny plate to fit in the back of radios. One thousand seven hundred plates a day. I wasn't badly paid and the place had the advantage of being on the riverbank. When I was ahead of my quota I could go out, smoke a cigarette, and watch the river—we were seven in the factory, seven with the boss and his son. Listening to the water, I decided how I was going to show Stepan where he could catch trout without being interfered with.

The only bad thing was the oil, it splattered my hands and wrists, I couldn't wear gloves for they slowed me down too much, and my skin was allergic to the oil. Little spots came up which itched. Stepan said that if the spots didn't go away within a week, by July 17th—I remember the date of each day of that month of summer skies, endless days, swallows, and the unimaginable—he would categorically forbid me to work there!

I kept my room at the widow's house and I spent every night IN EUROPA. On two Sundays when Stepan was working the day shift, I watched the swallows: on two Sundays when he wasn't working we stayed in bed till nightfall. He talked a lot now. In his sleep he talked in Russian. We'll stick it out another year, he said, then we'll leave and I'll find a job. You ought to make beds like this one! I told him. We'll find a house by the sea, he said. Why not by a lake? I suggested.

Sometimes he talked of the factory. I asked him if he'd heard about Michel's accident. I'd just arrived, he said, it was my first week and I was in his team. It was Peter we were tapping, and the wall broke. When that happens it's like hell let loose. Hell itself, my little one. To pierce the wall you have a probe—do you know how long the tip lasts? Less than eight minutes. *Vossiem.* He was still conscious. May God help him. We got him clear and put the fireproof gown on him. He's still in hospital, I commented. With two legs gone, said Stepan.

Towards evening he shaved. I liked watching him shave. We had a jug and basin on the table by the door and he went to fetch some hot water from the bathhouse, a stone building next to the shop. Naturally I never set foot inside there. Stepan would fetch water for me to wash, and for the calls of nature I went into the plantation. This time the water was for his shaving. How much I liked to watch him shave! Perhaps any man shaving? If I'd gone into the bathhouse I'd know. It's the only moment men show their coquetry. The way they pull their skin and focus with their eyes, the noise of the blade against the stubble, the white soap on the rosy skin. After shaving, Stepan's face was softer than mine, soft as a baby's.

He was killed on July 31st. He didn't take the leather-covered flask with him. He left it on the table beside his shaving brush. He was killed at four-thirty in the morning. Régis telephoned the news to the widow Besson's house just before I was leaving for work. I spoke to him myself. Is it certain he's dead? Certain? Certain? I asked six times. I went to work. The pieces I was pressing, tiny as earrings, were for electric irons. After work I went to the Barracks and into our room. There was a knock on the door. I opened it. Giuliano stood there. It was he who obtained the oak for our bed.

Where is he? I asked, I want to see him. *Niente*, Giuliano said. I want to see him, I said again very quietly. *Niente!* he shouted at the top of his voice. Over his shoulder I could see other men from shed A and sheds P, O, R, U, E, N standing at a discreet distance, looking towards me, caps in hand, shoulders hunched. Where is he? Giuliano's eyes filled with tears as he shook his head. Not for a moment did he take his eyes off me. And suddenly I understood. He had disappeared. There was no body. Like it happens in an avalanche.

I did not cry, Holy Mary Mother of God, I did not cry. I said to Giuliano: Who's got a motorbike in our shed? None of us. Who then? Jan in U has a motorbike. Ask him if he can take me to work tomorrow morning, I'm going to stay here.

I slept in our room. Every morning Jan took me to the Components Factory in Cluses. On the second day Emile came to the Barracks. We want you to come home, he said, and shyly, without a word, he deposited a goat's cheese on the table. Later, I told him, tell Maman and Régis I'll come home later, for the moment I must stay here.

I lay on the bed with the carved roses at each corner and stared at the planks of the roof. I found a suitcase under the bed and into it I packed his clothes, with no idea of what I was going to do with them. Perhaps his father or his wife would want them? I still did not cry. The nothingness into which he had disappeared filled me. Every hour was the same. Every minute was the same. To piss I went into the plantation just as I did when his boots weren't open mouths screaming. Odile did not scream, she waited. IN EUROPA, shed A. I went on waiting. Every evening some of his comrades came to see me. They came in pairs. They brought me plates of food which I couldn't eat. One brought me a newspaper in a language I couldn't understand. They said I should go home. They said they would come and see me if I went home. One of them gave me a lace shawl in black. I folded it up. Each day which passed brought me more hope. Each night I slept in the shed. In the nothingness into which he had disappeared, in the nothingness in which he had left me, I was listening for him. And at last I heard. Now I could go home, now I could weep, now I could wear my black shawl.

I went to the factory manager's office. His secretary asked me what my business was. I said it was private. Would you like to take a chair? I could hear the avalanche roar of the big furnaces. I knew that it never stopped, yet, as I sat there waiting, I thought it might. Impossible things happen. I believed that if the roar stopped I would hear his voice. On the walls were framed photographs of other factories. The frames were oak like the bed. I waited for an hour. He shouldn't be much longer, said the secretary. Where is he? He's on a long-distance call, she replied and continued her typing.

If I'd taken a back-of-the-arse, I could have done her job. Would you like some coffee? she asked. She knew me, everyone in the factory knew by now that I was Stepan Pirogov's concubine. It wasn't of course the word they used, but it was the legal term which I would have to use. Please, I said.

After another half-hour the manager saw me. His wife used to order fresh eggs from Mother. When Father was alive, Mother had to wait until he was in the fields before delivering her eggs. Food for the enemy! Father would have screamed.

He never looked at you when he was talking, the manager. It was as if he were trying to read the captions of the framed photographs on the wall. He had taken off his jacket and loosened his tie. It was hot everywhere with an August heat. I had put on a skirt and jacket so as to look more legal, and I was wearing the black shawl over my head. He motioned to the chair in front of him.

What can I do for you?

I've come about Monsieur Pirogov, Monsieur Norat.

I know. May I offer you, and the family, my sincere condolences.

I understand that if a worker is killed at work, the Company pays his wife a pension.

It is discretionary. We are not obliged to, and the pension terminates when and if the widow marries again.

Monsieur Pirogov was killed at work, I said.

The cause has not yet been ascertained.

Everyone knows he was asphyxiated by fumes. That's why he fell.

We will see, Mademoiselle Blanc, when the investigation is finished. I wish I could tell you more.

I have come to apply for a pension.

How old are you?

Seventeen.

And the date of your marriage, Mademoiselle Blanc? He
was obliged to look at me at that moment.

We are not married.

Then I don't understand.

I lived as Monsieur Pirogov's concubine.

May I ask where?

I knew he knew where.

In shed A, I told him.

That's company property.

I want our bed too.

You want a company pension and a bed! If we gave pen-
sions to all our workers' concubines. Mademoiselle Blanc,
we'd be bankrupt!

Are there so many killed in your factories, Monsieur Norat?

I understand your distress but I'm afraid I can do nothing.

I'm pregnant. In the name of his child which I'm carrying,
I'm asking, Sir, for compensation.

Monsieur Norat was surprised. He left his chair and came
to stand behind me.

Odile, if I may so call you, for you're young enough to be
my daughter, I believe you, but the Company can't. From the
Company's point of view you're not married, you had no fixed
residence of concubinage, and you have no proof at all that
Stepan Pirogov is the father of your child.

You were born, Christian, on April 10th. You weighed 3.4
kilos, you had blue eyes, hair softer than the thistledown of a
dandelion, hands smaller than Stepan's thumbs and legs like
holy bread, with a zizi between them.

My mother hoped to keep you at home and put you on a
bottle. I wanted to feed you myself. I had enough milk for
twins. The boss at the Components Factory was obliging: so
long as I did my quota, he wasn't fussy about clocking in and
out. I didn't have to wait, like the others, till midday. When I

felt my blouse wet on either side with milk, I left the machines thumping away and the metal shavings getting higher and higher on the shop floor. How you sucked! How you loved life! Then I had to get back early to sweep up the shavings and start again on tiny pieces for airplane hatches.

You were nearly a year old. You were taking your first steps on the earth, and after the fourth you'd fall back onto your bottom. Funny to think of this in the sky.

Emile was playing with you under the table. Régis had been out the night before and had drunk too much. It's not the worst men who drink, the men who drink are the frightened ones, they don't know of what, we're all frightened, though at the age of eighteen I didn't know any of this. Régis was arguing with Emile, who was under the table playing with you, about whether Corneille the cattle dealer's Peugeot was dark blue or black. Emile was sure it was black. Régis was sure it was blue. They went on and on. Stop it! I cried out. You're worse than children! Régis swung round so fast I thought he was going to hit me. You keep out of this! he said. You've got enough of your own business to mind, Odile! Better think what you're going to do with your poor bastard of a kid! Shut your mouth! Emile seized Régis's legs and he fell to the ground. At that moment Mother walked in and the three of us pretended nothing had happened. When Mother left, Régis, his head in his hands, a smear of blood under his nose, muttered: Blue, Corneille's Peugeot is blue! I'm going for a walk, I said.

I walked along the rail track towards the Heaps. The last one was smoking. Soon they'll be as high as the factory, I thought. Soon they'll have covered our orchard, I thought. At home there are only three cows left. There's nothing more dead in the world than this dirt left over after burning at two thousand centigrade. Twenty-two months down in the dirt is the bastard's father. I had the courage to say those words to myself.

Every time I go over there to work, Giuliano the Sardinian told me after Stepan's death, I'm not sure I'm going to come back.

Each wall, each opening, each ladder was like the bone of a sheep's skull found in the mountain—fleshless, emptied, extinct. The furnaces throbbed, the river flowed, the smoke, sometimes white, sometimes grey, sometimes yellow, thrust upwards into the sky, men worked night and day for generations, sweating, retching, pissing, coughing, the Factory had not stopped once for seven years, it produced thirty thousand tons of ferromanganese a year, it made money, it tested new alloys, it made experiments, it made profits, and it was inert, barren, derelict. I went through the melting shop where the furnace for manganese oxide is in the sky, and Peter and Tito for the ferromanganese are well below it, yet still so high that when the coasting cranes teem their metal into the ladles, you squint up at the ladles like suns setting, and I knew how the womb in my belly was the opposite of all I could see and touch. Here's a woman, I whispered, and the fruit of her womb. I knelt on my knees. Nobody saw me.

Horse leather is the best leather for gloves, Dilenka, it resists the heat.

I climbed up eight metal ladders, each one as high as hay in a barn, nobody stopped me, to the manganese-oxide furnace. This is where he fell. The fumes hurt my throat and I breathed deeply, yet nothing happened. I came down the eight ladders. I crossed the office space that had been the Ram's Ballroom. I found the locker where he kept his horse-leather gloves and his blue shield. It had an Italian name on it now. I laughed. I surprised myself laughing. Our love was imperishable.

Across the footbridge we lived IN EUROPA. The river was low, for the thaw had not begun. On many days it was minus ten and the mountains were still imprisonned. There was no time, I was thinking as I watched the water of the Giffre, to show Stepan where to take the trout, only time for Stepan and Odile to meet and for Christian to be conceived. Upstream, between the rocks, something attracted my attention. I waited. It seemed to me that it turned its head. A lorry clattered along the road and it flew up, long legs dangling, to perch in a pine tree. It was a heron. A water bird that nests in the top of a tree, said Stepan. I've seen three herons in my life so far. One with Father when I was small enough for him to carry me, one with Stepan on a June evening, and one that Sunday in March '56.

Stepan said the name of the heron was *tzaplia*, a creature from far away with a message. Waiting for its fish, it becomes as still as a stick. Which is why I wasn't sure when I first spotted it. From the pine tree the heron surveyed the road, the factory grounds, the tall chimneys with their heads like the open beaks of gigantic fledgelings looking up for food, the manganese-oxide furnace, Peter, Tito, the turbine house, the cliff-face and tht sky where I'm flying with my son. Of its message I was ignorant.

She was in a good mood, Mother. She gave us a kilo of honey, she said your blue eyes were going to break girls' hearts, she changed your nappies. For once I wasn't in a hurry to leave and we missed the bus back to Cluses and had to hitch-hike. You made hitchhiking easy. With you in my arms, the very first car stopped. The driver leant back and opened the rear door. As we were climbing in, he spoke my name. He was wearing a cap over his eyes and he had a black beard. Yet something in the way he said my name was familiar, was old. Our eyes met and suddenly I recognised him.

Michel!

He leant his head back awkwardly for me to kiss his cheek. I guessed he couldn't turn round, couldn't move his legs, so I kissed him like that.

I was so sorry, Odile, when I heard about what happened, he said. I offer you my sympathy and all my condolences.

His voice had changed. Changed more than his face on account of his beard. Before, he had spoken like most people do, his voice close-up to what he was saying. Now his voice was far away, like a priest's voice at the altar.

This is our son, Christian, I told him.

He touched your woolen bonnet with his hand and it was then I noticed the scars on it: they were violet—the same colour as molybdenum bread goes when it's cooling. Where they were violet, there was less flesh.

You're going where? he asked.

Cluses.

You live there?

I nodded. And you, Michel?

Lyons's finished with me. The surgeons say I'm a master-piece. Do you know how many operations I had? Thirty-seven!

He laughed and slapped his thigh so the sound should remind me it was made of metal. He was wearing well-pressed trousers, light-coloured socks, polished shoes.

You started to cry.

Developing his lungs! said Michel. He can't run at his age, poor little mite, all he can do is to howl if he wants to fill his lungs. Here! Christian! Look!

He dangled a key-ring before your eyes and you leant your head against my breast and stopped crying.

And you, Michel?

I'm going to take on the tobacconist's and newspaper shop at Pouilly.

How will you manage to—

Everything, Odile, everything. I can even climb a ladder! The trade union lawyers forced them to give me a pension. I don't have to work too much.

Stupidly, helplessly and for no good reason, I began to

snivel. Michel turned round and started the engine. He could drive the car, for it had been adapted and fitted out with hand-controls. His two feet in their polished shoes just rested on the floor. Like flatirons.

When there's no choice, Michel said over his shoulder, it's extraordinary what you can adapt to.

I know.

At first I was too drugged to realise, he said, then bit by bit the truth came home to me. When I woke up in the morning and remembered what I was, I wanted to scream. For a week I was in despair. Why me? I kept on asking. Why me?

I know, I said. You'd gone to sleep. We were driving along by the river. He controlled the speed with his scarred right hand. His two feet lay on the floor like flatirons. I was still sniffling.

The great thing in hospital is you aren't alone. There are other people in the same state as you, he said, some are worse off than you. You've only got one life, they say, so better make the most of it. It's not true, Odile.

I know, I said between tears.

We were all bad cases. Third-degree burns, with fifty, sixty, seventy percent disability. We'd have all been dead twenty years ago. There were people—we heard it—there were people who said we'd be better off dead. We had to learn to live a second life. The first one was over forever and ever. He's sleeping now?

He's asleep, yes, I whispered.

I had to learn how to live—and it wasn't like learning for the second time, that's what's so strange, Odile, it was like learning for the first time. Now I'm beginning my second life.

Do you have much pain? I asked.

Not much.

Never?

Not much. Sometimes when it's hot in the summer I'm uncomfortable. He touched the top of his thigh. Otherwise, no. For a long while I dreamt of pain in my legs. They weren't amputated in my dreams. I'll tell you something else, Odile. I've become a fire-cutter.

I started to laugh. As with my tears, I didn't know why.

There was an old man in the hospital. He wasn't a patient and he wasn't a member of the staff . . . he was there every day. He went out to buy whatever we asked him—papers, fruit, tobacco, eau de cologne—and in return we gave him the change. He was eighty-two. When he was younger he'd been a railwayman. He was a fire-cutter. I saw him take the pain away once. A nurse scalded her hands with boiling water, and the old man put a stop to her suffering in two minutes. According to him he was getting too old, said the effort of cutting the fire took too much out of him. So, one day he announced he'd been watching us all very carefully and now he'd decided, now he'd chosen his successor. And it was to be me. He gave me his gift.

How?

Like that.

What did he do?

He just gave me his gift.

We were in Cluses and Michel drove us to the front door. You were already asleep in my arms. Despite my protests he insisted on getting out of the car. He moved his legs with his arms. He pulled himself up with his arms. His neck and shoulders were much thicker than they had been. He extracted himself like a man climbing out of a trench he's dug. There he stood on the pavement, swaying slightly from his hips.

If you ever need me, you know where to find me now. I was so sorry, he repeated again, to hear what had happened.

Do you remember Stepan? I asked him.

I remember him. He was very tall, with blond hair. Didn't

he have blue eyes? We worked a couple of nights in the same gang, two or three nights I think—before I collected this packet. He slapped his hip.

I don't even have a picture of him, I said.

You don't need a photo, he said, fingering your woolen bonnet, you have his progeny.

Strange word, progeny!

You can't have closer, he said. Good night.

The long years began, the long years of your boyhood. Do you remember the flat we lived in? You did your homework on the kitchen table. You were always wanting me to make potato pancakes for supper. You kept a soccer ball in a net hung from the ceiling over your bed. Your room smelt of glue because of the models you made. The same smell as my nail varnish. You could change washers on a tap before you were ten. In my room there was the oak bed with the carved roses, when you were ill you slept in it with me and sometimes on Sundays too. Remember when we painted the living room and you fell off the ladder? You were all I had in the world and I thought you were dead.

Why do I have the same name as you, Maman, why am I called Christian Blanc?

Because your father died before you were born.

What was he like?

Strong.

What did he look like?

Big.

Was he like me?

Yes.

Was he interested in aircraft?

Not particularly, I think.

You don't know much about him, do you?

As much as anyone ever knows.

Guess what I really want to do, Maman. I want to build a glider. One that will fly. I saw a picture in a book at school. It'll have to be big, as big as a car.

Big enough to fly us round the world?

Yes . . . I'll need lots of glue.

The long years began. Where could we go to be at home? Régis got married to Marie-Jeanne. Her condition for marrying him was that he give up drinking, and for a while he did. Mother sold the last cow, keeping only the goats and chickens. The trees of the forest, up by the path to Le Mont, began to die. The hillside above the river became the grey rusty colour of dead wood. Emile got a job loading drums in a paint factory near the frontier and Mother lavished all her attention upon him. Every evening he came home to a hero's welcome. His weaknesses inspired her determination to live to be a hundred. As she aged, Emile became the love of her life. She changed the hay of his mattress every week.

I bought an atlas to study how to go to Stockholm. I found the Ukraine and the river Pripiat. Yet what could we have done there? We'd have been further from home than ever.

Why are we going up so fast now?

The boss at the Components Factory pursued us for a while. You remember he bought you a Sputnik with a dog inside, and you lost the dog? I went to his house for supper several times. He took us to the lake and we ate a fish like a trout but stronger tasting. You said fish find their way in the ocean through their sense of smell. His wife had left him years before. He was nearly forty, you were nine.

Do you want to marry Gaston, Maman?

We are still climbing into the sky.

No, I don't want to marry him.

I think he wants to marry you.

I don't know.

He told me he's going to buy a Citroën DS.

That's what interests you, isn't it?

If you didn't have to work for him, Maman, I think I'd like him more.

Gaston is very kind. He and I don't know the same things, that's all. What he knows doesn't interest me a lot and what I know would frighten him.

You couldn't frighten me, Maman.

When we turn, Christian, it's strange, for there I am looking not up but down at the blue sky.

Michel's shop in Pouilly was unlike any other in the district. The newspapers were arranged in a special way, the left-wing ones always in front. When a customer asked for *Le Figaro*, Michel bent down and brought one up from under the counter with a look of disgust, as if the paper the man had demanded were wrapped round a rotten fish. He sold bottles of gnôle with a pear the size of my fist inside the bottle.

How did the pear get inside? you asked.

It grew from a pip! Michel said and you didn't know whether to believe him or not.

He also sold toboggans and radios. He was mad about radios and could repair anything. On the back wall of the shop he pinned a large map of the world and on each country he stuck little labels like the ones they sell for jam pots, indicating the city, the wavelength, the hours of broadcasting. There were those who said that Michel with his politics and his radios could only be a spy for the Russians! His reputation as a fire-cutter spread. People from other valleys came to him to have the pain of their burns taken away. He categorically refused any payment. It's a gift! he repeated.

Do you remember when I took you to him? You'd burnt the palm of your hand with a firecracker. It wasn't serious but you were howling your head off. Michel came out from

behind the counter with his stiff, swaying movement—like a
skittle. Let's go into the back room, he said. I made as if to
accompany you but he shook his head and the two of you
disappeared. He closed the door and within seconds you
stopped howling. Not gradually but suddenly in mid-cry.
There wasn't a sound in the shop. Total silence. After what
seemed an eternity I couldn't bear it anymore and shouted
your name. You came bounding through the door laughing.
Michel lumbered after you. There were already grey hairs in
his black head.

You don't have to burn yourself in order to come and see
me, he said when I thanked him and kissed him good-bye.

Later I asked you: What happened?

Nothing.

What did Michel do?

He showed me one of his burns.

Where?

Here—you pointed at your tummy.

And your hand stopped hurting?

No, it wasn't hurting anymore. It stopped hurting before
he showed me his burn.

Why did he show it to you then?

Because I asked him.

What are we doing here, Christian, on this earth, in this
sky?

I'd been working in the Components Factory for ten years.
On the wall beside my bench there were thirty postcards of
the Mediterranean and palm trees and cows and cherry trees
in flower and a village with a steeple—all of them sent to
me over the years by friends on holiday. Gaston had understood the reality of our situation. When he stood behind me,
pretending to oversee my work, I could sense his regret in my
shoulder blades, because I could also sense my own. The

racket of the machines month after month, year after year, wore away principles. The years were long. When I didn't sleep the nights too were long.

The factory shut for the month of August. We never went away for a holiday like some of the others. I gave Mother a hand in the garden. I made jam and bottled the last of the runner beans. When I passed the factory I no longer thought of Stepan. There is nothing in the factory which can have a memory. I thought of him when I ironed your shirts and cut your hair. I thought of him too when I did my face in the mirror. I was ageing. I looked as though I'd been married for twenty years.

Do you know how to measure a smile? Stepan asked.

Yes, I said.

He bent down and picked me up so my mouth was level with his and he kissed me.

You had a friend called Sébastien, whose father was the care-taker of the holiday camp in Bakon, on the other side of the Roc d'Enfer. Some Thursdays when there was no school, you spent the day with him up there. I was glad because the mountain air did you good. Cluses is like a dungeon. When the holiday camp was full of kids from the cities in the north, you wanted to go and find out if there were any flying enthusiasts. Here, you said, people don't have a clue. Already I couldn't follow you talking about "aerofoils" and "wing loadings." I'm not sure Sébastien understood much either. His passion was fiddling with television sets. He could come into Michel's shop and talk like a schoolmaster for an hour about new transistor circuits. Sébastien was twelve and you were eleven when in August '66 you went to spend a whole fort-night with him up in Bakon.

I didn't have to go to work and I was by myself, alone as I hadn't been for ten years. On the second day I did something

I hadn't done since Stepan's death: I didn't get dressed at all,
I lay in bed, I listened to the radio, I took a shower when I
was too hot, I remembered, I didn't get up. Mother would
have been deeply ashamed of me. Papa, examining the cruel
crevices in his hands, would have looked up and said with a
wink: Why not, if she can? My life already seemed inexplicably long. The next day I spent at the swimming pool
sunbathing. From having to stand too much at work I was
developing varicose veins. My hands weren't like Papa's but
they were red and rough. I was never taught to swim. I made
an appointment at the hairdresser's. Mother had never once
been to a hairdresser in her life.

Coming out of the hairdresser's with a scarf over my head,
I saw Michel on the other side of the road. He was walking
on crutches. I waved and he didn't see me. His head was
down and it looked as though the going was painful. I waited
for the traffic and then I ran across the street. When at last
he saw me, his face, red and glistening with sweat, broke
into a smile.

What a surprise! Always in his faraway voice.

I've just had my hair done.

Come and have a coffee.

We went to the brasserie by the post office. A waiter offered
him a chair. Obstinately he took another.

Why don't you take off your scarf?

Order me a café au lait and I'll be back. I went to the toilet.

Ah! Odile! A beautiful head of hair you have there! All his
words had to be hurled across the ravine of what had befallen
him.

It's too fine. It breaks too easily.

Too fine? I wouldn't know what too fine was! He drank
from his glass of white wine and lemonade. You remember
the trip we made to Italy?

I nodded.

Thirteen years ago.

The only time I've ever been on a motorbike. Afterwards you told me I was a good passenger.

Your outfit has closed down for the whole month?

Like every year.

What about a trip to Paris?

Paris! It's hundreds of kilometres away.

We take the car and we take four days, there and back. I have to go anyway to get a prosthesis adjusted. It's not satisfactory . . . the left one here. If you came with me, it would be a holiday. What do you say?

It's a long way.

Don't put your scarf on again.

Are we, Christian, a mother and child flying in the sky?

At that moment I was twenty-nine; Michel was thirty-seven. If I'd been told as a child what the life of an adult is like, I wouldn't have believed it. I'd never have believed it could be so unfinished. When young we lend so much authority and sureness to our elders. Michel and I had seen and lived a good deal, and yet, as we followed the Rhône along the gorge through the end of the Jura Mountains, we were like children. When I think of it now, I want to protect us.

It was a white Renault 4. He had covered the seats with a fabric, striped like a zebra skin. He liked putting on a strong eau de cologne which, mixed with sweat and the August heat, smelt like mule. I'd bought a pair of white net gloves for the trip. In my whole life I never dreamt of wearing gloves in the summer but I'd seen this pair in a shop in Cluses, a shop where the bosses' wives bought their haberdashery, and I said to myself: What the hell, Odile, if you're going to Paris, Paris of all places on this earth, and you've got a smart pair of white shoes, you may as well wear white net gloves in August. In addition, they were at half-price.

When I think of us on our way to Paris, I want us to come to no harm.

The white cat died last week. She was hit by a car. Michel was at the shop and I went out into the garden and I heard a meow. She was in the grass by the edge of the road. Her back was broken, so I put her to lie on a blanket by the stove in the kitchen. She lay there, her white mouth a little open and her tongue scarcely less white than her teeth. She turned —or her body turned her—onto her side with her four legs stretched out and her hind legs straight behind her, as if she were leaping. Slowly, with her two forelegs she wiped her face, moving her paws down from her ears over her eyes towards her mouth. She did this once only, rubbing the vision of life out of her eyes. When her paws reached her mouth she was dead.

Can there be any love without pity?

The Jura are not like our mountains. They are more morose, more resigned to their fate. They would never cover a car seat with zebra skin nor wear white gloves in August. We passed a lake which looked as though no boat had ever sailed upon it. Michel talked about General de Gaulle and I didn't know whether he hated or admired him. Next he talked about the factory. It belonged now to a multinational with factories in twenty-one different countries. TPI. The multinationals, Michel said, are the new robber barons of our time. TPI made eight thousand five hundred million francs profit in '66.

Michel keeps figures in his head like other people keep the words of songs.

> It's raining kisses
> and hailing caresses
> till the flood of tenderness
> takes the nest.

A man on one of their furnaces, he said, breathes air that contains four hundred thousand dust particles per litre—that's lethal.

May a mouthful of this on your night shift my darling keep you company between the hot and the cold . . .

Lethal. No man can stand it indefinitely, Michel said. The forest is dying. The five chimneys spew out one thousand two hundred tons of fluorine waste every year.

Papa had been right about the venom. He had been right too about my being married at seventeen. What he never knew, what he could never have imagined, was that I'd be a widow by eighteen.

A TPI factory in the Pyrenees, Michel went on, has destroyed four thousand hectares of forest in three years and poisoned seven hundred and fifty cows and sheep.

What I've lost is more than seven hundred and fifty cows and sheep! I said.

You have a child. It helps.

It helps, yes, but a son doesn't make up for everything. One day he'll go.

At least you have somebody to live for.

Sometimes, I shouted, you want to live for yourself!

We each have to live for ourselves, he said.

Sometimes I look at other women and I hate them because they're, because they're . . .

Not living with a ghost?

I'm getting out, let me get out.

You have nothing to be angry about.

Nobody has the right to call him a ghost. Do you hear me, Michel? Nobody. He's here! I beat my hand on my breast.

And I'm here, Michel said banging his hands down on the steering wheel, I'm here and I have no child so I know what I'm saying when I tell you you're lucky.

Lucky? Me lucky! I'm about as lucky as you, my dear Michel.

He said nothing more. We were driving between hills of grass which rose to outcrops of rock. The sky was thundery. The cows were clustered together, heads down, wherever there was a little shade. We were both sweating and hot.

If you see a river, I said, why don't you stop? Then I remembered it would be hard for him to clamber down a river-bank and I regretted saying it. Can you still have children? I asked him after five minutes' silence.

He nodded without a word.

Around the next corner was a café and we stopped. We were waiting for the sandwich we had ordered when we heard a screeching of brakes followed by a crash. I rushed to the café door. A Peugeot 304, coming too fast round the bend, had crashed into the back of our Renault. The driver, unhurt, was waving his arms and cursing everything he could see. In God's name, it's not possible! No warning for the bend! How is it possible to build such a fool road? And to park a car there you need the mind of a cunt! It's not possible, Jesus, I'm telling you it's not possible!

Michel walked over to his car and bent stiffly forward from the waist; he was like the conductor of a brass band after the end of a number, and he examined the damage. The other driver was pacing out the distance from the two cars to the corner and counting out loud in a shrill, mad voice. He had a way of looking at things, Michel—shafts, flanges, joints, cylinder heads, casings—which stopped them being intransigent, which made them obedient. As I watched him I thought of his gift of taking away the pain of burns. Was it a gift of attracting to himself and so dispersing a kind of shock? The shock suffered by burnt flesh or a chassis?

If we order the parts tonight, he shouted to me, it's only one day's work, we'll be on the road the day after tomorrow.

Swaying like a ninepin, he moved across to the Peugeot. The owner screamed: It's not possible! Less than twenty-eight metres from the corner, you can see my brake marks, can't you? Jesus! I jammed them on as soon as I saw you. You're a public danger. If you're a gimp you should get yourself about in a wheelchair.

I reckon, said Michel very calmly, the packet there won't cost you more than a hundred and fifty thousand—the price of a good bicycle! You're fortunate, considering the speed you were going.

Crippled cunt! the man said.

The storm hadn't broken and we had to wait for the café owner to drive us to the nearest hotel, five kilometres away.

Give us some cold beer, can you? Michel asked. The sweat lined the furrows of his brow and the pouches under his eyes. He sat on a table, his back to the wall, legs straight out, pointed polished shoes at an impossible angle, as if both ankles were broken.

On a day like this, he said to me, when you're working on the furnaces, you're working in a temperature of seventy degrees centigrade. Halfway between blood-heat and boiling point. Halfway to hell . . . He poured some beer down his throat.

I could never believe in hell, I told him. I couldn't believe any father would invent hell as a punishment for his children.

Fathers shoot their sons dead, he said.

They shoot in anger. The way I learnt, hell has to do with justice, not anger.

I offered him a handkerchief to wipe his face. He held it up before his eyes because it had flowers printed on it, and he didn't use it.

You really want to know about hell, he said smiling, it's here.

Sounds odd coming from you, Michel, the one who's always talking about change and progress . . .

I put the handkerchief carefully back in my bag.

Who says hell has to stay the same? Hell begins with hope. If we didn't have any hopes we wouldn't suffer. We'd be like those rocks against the sky.

I caught hold of the hand he was pointing with. He didn't resist and I turned it over. On the back of his fingers he has black hairs; where the violet scar is, there is no hair. I sprayed some eau de cologne onto his wrist and he withdrew his hand to smell it.

Hell begins with the idea that things can be made better, he said. It's refreshing—your scent. What's the opposite of hell? Paradise, no?

Give me your other hand.

I sprayed the back of that hand and he didn't withdraw it, it lay in my lap.

I could take you to your hotel now, announced the café owner.

The hotel backed onto a river whose bed was almost dry. The window of my room looked out onto the pebbles. It was the first time in my life I'd stayed in a hotel—which didn't prevent my realising this one was unusual. The proprietor, who was working in the kitchen when we arrived, came out wiping his hands on a sack tied round his waist.

Two rooms, yes, he said, you'll be eating here tonight? Tonight I'm cooking a dish I've never tried before!

The corridor leading to the bedrooms was stacked with wardrobes, there was scarely space to get by. In my room, besides a bed and a washbasin there were two electric radiators and a deep freeze. I looked inside the freezer and it was full of meat. At last the rain began to fall, large drops the size of pearls. I washed and lay on the bed in my slip, with my feet bare.

I had the impression that we had lost our way: we were not going to arrive in Paris, Michel's prosthesis was not going to be adjusted, we were in a land apart, which we had come across by accident, without meaning to, and without realising it, until now we had found ourselves in a hotel run by a madman. With this idea, and yet peacefully and to the sound of the rain, I fell asleep.

When I woke up the storm had passed. I put on another dress and a pair of white shoes—the pair which had prompted me to buy the summer gloves. I also put on a necklace of coloured beads that Christian had made for me at school. It was getting dark—the short days of August for all their heat—and I could just make out the white shapes of geese down by the river. I slipped past the wardrobes and found my way downstairs.

To my surprise there were three or four other guests in the dining room. Michel was sitting at a table by the window, where there was a large vase of orange gladioli. I can still see the flowers. He had changed his shirt and washed.

So too had the proprietor, who had discarded the sack and was now wearing a tie. He led me to the table. Michel insisted upon getting to his feet. We said good evening to each other like people do in films.

Would we like an aperitif? asked the proprietor. Two Suzes, said Michel. My sense of us having lost our way reminded me of the uncertainty children feel when they find themselves having to do something for the first time. Yet I'd never felt older.

Can we propose to you, sir, poularde en soutien-gorge?

What is it? asked Michel.

A skinned chicken roasted in pastry, sir. Unforgettable. And as an entrée perhaps truite au bleu?

It's the chicken you've cooked this way for the first time? I asked.

Precisely, Madame, the first soutien-gorge I've ever fitted! he winked at Michel.

Four point to the sky, four walk in the dew, and four have food in them; all twelve make one—what is it? I asked the man.

He didn't know and I wouldn't tell him. We ate well, like at a baptism.

If you wanted, I could help you, Michel said.

What do I need help for?

To live.

I've managed not too badly up to now. It's good, this white wine, isn't it? Santé.

Do you know what people say about you?

I've never worried. It's the one thing, Michel, I've never worried about.

There's no talking with her, they say. When Odile's made up her mind to do something, she does it. When she's made up her mind not to, nothing can make her. There's no approaching her. They respect your courage, they respect the way you've brought up the boy—but from a distance. You're alone.

I don't feel it.

In a few years it'll be too late.

Too late for what?

Too late to change.

You want to change everything, Michel, the world, hell, people, politics, now me.

You think things can stay as they are?

I don't know.

Happiness doesn't say anything to you?

There's more pain than happiness, I said.

Pain, yes.

Have I told you the story of the two bears? I asked.

Who's been eating from my plate? The story of the three bears?

No, two. Two bears in the snow . . .

Fairy tales, Odile! We're too old now for fairy tales. We need to face reality.

Like we both do all the time.

Then he said something that impressed me, for he said it so slowly and emphatically: Things can't . . . go on . . . as they are. These words were more grunted than spoken and the gladioli I was gazing at in their vase blurred before my eyes.

They do go on, I replied, every day, every hour. People work, people go home to eat, feed the cat, watch TV, go to bed, make jam, mend radios, take baths, it all goes on all the while—till one day each of us dies.

And that's what you're waiting for! he said.

I'm not waiting for anything.

You know you talk like an old woman?

I'm a widow. I was a widow at eighteen.

You talk like an old woman and you're not thirty.

In three months. Very soon. You believe age makes a difference?

It's not age, it's time running out. He dabbed at his forehead with his red handkerchief.

Say it again, Michel, I taunted him, according to you things can't go on. But they do—you know it as well as I do. Things go on!

If we don't fight, he said, we lose all.

Do you really think life's only a battle?

At this he laughed, laughed till the tears came to his eyes. He filled up my glass, raised his, and we clinked them.

You of all people, Odile, not to know the answer to that question. Do you—you, Odile Blanc—really think life isn't a battle?

He laughed shortly again but this time his tears were those of sadness.

When I went up to my room, with the freezer full of meat and a reproduction of the Angelus above the bed, I didn't undress. I waited for half an hour and watched the river. Then I brushed my hair and, without putting my shoes on, I edged my way past the wardrobes in the corridor and found the door to Michel's room, which I opened without knocking.

Our shadow is moving over the white snow, Christian, and looks like the twenty-seventh letter of the alphabet, something between a *D* and an *L*. In Cluses, where I learnt words off the blackboard in the school, which, after the factory, was the tallest building I'd ever seen, in Cluses words were strange to me. Now they are coming back into my head like pigeons into their pigeon loft.

From our union, Marie-Noelle was born on 4 August '67. At birth she weighed 3.2 kilos, a little less than you. The milk came up into my breasts and I fed her for more than nine months. I didn't want to stop. I was no longer working in the Components Factory, for the four of us lived together above the shop in Pouilly.

Madame Labourier knitted a pink blanket for the cradle. Odile Blanc was not exactly the daughter-in-law Madame Labourier would have chosen for her son, but facts were facts, and Marie-Noelle was her granddaughter.

When Michel was young, Madame Labourier informed me, you couldn't count the number of girls he went out with. After the accident, during the years he was away in Lyons, they all got married. All things considered, it's understandable, isn't it? After all, *they* were young healthy girls.

Later she warned me about the future. As he ages, he's

going to change, he's going to become more and more demanding. I saw it with Neighbour Henri who had polio, and my poor cousin Gervais who had diabetes. As they get older, cripples—particularly men cripples—become difficult and crotchety. You'll have to be patient, my girl.

After you were born, Marie-Noelle, it was as if you gave him back his legs. He was so proud of you, his pride had feet. He hated being separated from you for more than an hour or two. When you were old enough to go to school, he refused to take the car, he walked with you a good half-kilometre, holding your hand.

The limbs he had lost were somehow returned to him in your small child's body. It was he, not me, who taught you to walk. Now you are no longer a child and from the sky I can talk to you.

Women are beautiful when young, almost all women. Don't listen to envious gossip, Marie-Noelle. Whatever the proportions of a face, whether a body is too skinny or too heavy, at some moment a woman possesses the power of beauty which is given to us as women. Often the moment is brief. Sometimes the moment may come and we not even know it. Yet traces of it remain. Even at my advanced age now there are traces.

Look in a mirror if you pass one this afternoon in the hearing aid shop in Annecy whilst you're waiting for Papa, look at your hair which you washed last night and see how it invites being touched. Look at your shoulder when you wash at the sink and then look down at where your breast assembles itself, look at the part between shoulder and breast which slopes like an alpage—for thirty years still this slope is going to attract tears, teeth clenched in passion, feverish children, sleeping heads, work-rough hands. This beauty which hasn't a name. Look at how gently your stomach falls at its centre into the navel, like a white begonia in full bloom. You can touch its

beauty. Our hips move with an assurance that no man has;
yet they promise a peace, our hips, like a cow's tongue for
her calf. This frightens men, who knock us over and call
us cunts. Do you know what our legs are like, seen from the
back, Marie-Noelle, like lilies just before they open!

I will tell you which men deserve our respect. Men who
give themselves to hard labour so that those close to them can
eat. Men who are generous with everything they own. And
men who spend their lives looking for God. The rest are
pigshit.

Men aren't beautiful. Nothing has to stay in them. Nothing
has to be attracted by any peace they offer. So they're not
beautiful. Men have been given another power. They burn.
They give off light and warmth. Sometimes they turn night
into day. Often they destroy everything. Ashes are men's
stuff. Milk is ours.

Once you've learnt to judge for yourself and are no more
fooled by their boasts, it's not hard to tell the man who deserves
respect and the man who is pigshit. Yet the power of a man to
burn, we discover only by loving him. Does our love release
the power? Not always. I loved Stepan for many weeks before
we lived IN EUROPA. He was burning when I met him
on the footbridge.

Michel I started to love when we returned to the village.
We never got to Paris. I can die happily without seeing the
capital. We stayed for three nights at the mad hotel with the
white geese and his room opposite the wardrobes. Then we
came home.

Once in the factory Stepan and Michel worked on the same
shift for three days, yet it's in me they still meet. Marie-Noelle,
Christian—embrace each other tonight, whatever happens,
do this tonight, and know your fathers are embracing each
other.

It is getting late and the light is already turning. The snow on the Gruvaz, facing west, is turning pink, the colour of the best rhubarb when cooked. I imagined we would come down to earth before it's dark, but Christian must know what he's doing. He's a national instructor, he came second in the European Championship of Hang-gliding and when I said to him, they've both gone to Annecy, they needn't know anything, need they? they won't be frightened, take me up this afternoon, the time's come, he simply replied: Are you ready?

Strange how I'm not cold. I can feel each toe and each finger, they're warm as they were when I was a baby—I suddenly remember.

You take a man right into you and you cannot compare him or measure him or make a story of him. Everything that has ever been is swelling with the lips of the mouth into which you take him and he fills you, where you know as little as you know about an unborn child in your womb.

You can tell yourself other things about him when he has left, yet all of it remains far away compared to the places within you to which you lead him. Hay in the barn cannot change back into grass. If he's burning, the places to which you have led him are flooded with light. In your belly there are stars and of these stars you may be a victim. Poor Clotilde gave birth in the stable all alone, the door locked on the outside by her father.

It is painful for us to judge the man we have taken, for he's ours, already like a son. How can you judge a body which has been where he has been, who has come from there? Beside his single name all else is dead coals. How reluctant we are to judge! If we have to, if we are forced to, if we are picked up by the ears like a rabbit, we judge him and suffer the pain, the violence done to the sky within us where the stars shone. Men, poor men, judge more easily.

I never judged the life Stepan led before the Ram's Run.

All that happened before the 31st of December 1953 was beyond judgement or comparison, for it had brought him to me in shed A, IN EUROPA. Since his disappearance, he has stayed with me where I first took him and hid him, beyond ashes. He has stayed with me as the seasons stay with the world.

The furnaces which robbed Stepan of his life took away from Michel his legs and now they are taking away his hearing. At night when he unfastens the prostheses he is legless. The two stumps are the colour of molybdenum bread when it's cooling before the spray rains on it. Only their colour is like molybdenum. The specific gravity of molybdenum, Michel once told me, is 95.5—one of the heaviest metals, less heavy though than uranium, tungsten or lead. Legless, he weighs fifty-nine kilos. The colour alone of the stumps is like molybdenum, for they, unlike that monstrous metal, are alive. I know with my fingertips where their tissue is sensitive and the nerves murmur, and where the scarred flesh is numb, giving off warmth and taking in no sensation. On his back are light scars where they took skin to graft onto his face. Perhaps you are kissing my arse! he joked once when I was licking by his ear.

Without his artificial legs he hops like a bird on crutches. There are evenings when he lets me serve him like a king. Other times he is irritable and glowering and he pushes me away and, seizing his crutches, hops round the room like a plucked turkey. If he hears footsteps, when he's doing this, he flings himself onto the bed and pulls the sheet up to his grey beard. He has never let his daughter see him unharnessed. Passionately he wants his daughter to have an unmutilated father.

The wind is ruffling the sheet and the sheet is slapping like the washing in the orchard of my childhood when the bise blew. It won't blow away, Christian, are you sure?

Often the burnt come to the shop to have their pain taken away. Michel insists on being alone with them, I have never seen what he does. Sometimes somebody asks him to go down to an accident in the factory. Once or twice he has succeeded in taking the pain away by telephone. Four years ago, Louis's son, Gérard, was pruning an apple tree with a chain saw, standing on a ladder. Somehow he slipped and the chain saw, still turning, touched his neck before clattering to the ground. Blood was pouring out of a jugular vein into his shirt. He came running into the shop, his face like a sheep's. Michel stopped the bleeding within a minute without touching the wound. Then he sent Gérard down to the doctor, who couldn't believe his medical eyes.

Each time he takes away the pain he is exhausted afterwards, and, when I'm there, I massage the back of his neck and shoulders to give him relief. One night when I was doing this to him, he said: Paradise is rest, isn't it? Repose. You go to paradise after you've worked three shifts running, twenty-four hours without a break. You stop and there's the pure pleasure of stopping, doing nothing, lying down. Paradise is doing fuck-all. You don't know anything else exists. No relations in paradise, Odile, no children, no women, no men. Undistilled egotism, paradise! Isn't that it, my love? I went on massaging him and I felt his cart-horse shoulders relaxing, accepting. After a while he turned towards me, his eyes piercing me, and he pronounced my name. Then he took me in his arms, and he carried me, yes, he carried me to the bed and murmured: It's only in hell, my love, that we find each other!

And Michel found me there on the bed. He found Odile.

Look, look down there—can you see?—there's a heron flying. *Tzaplia*, the last message before nightfall.

Tell them, Christian, tell them when we land on the earth that there's nothing more to know.

PLAY
ME
SOMETHING

What is it that men have and women don't and which is hard and long?

On your left is the city of Verona, announced the bus driver over the loudspeaker. Verona was conquered by the Ostrogoths, later by the Barbarians, and still later by the Austrians. In the fourteenth century Verona was the setting of the love story between Romeo and Juliet.

What is it that men have and women don't and which is hard and long?

Tell us! demanded the boys.

Military service!

The flatness of the surrounding countryside was unfamiliar, making it difficult to judge distances. The coach was traveling fast, yet it seemed that time passed and nothing changed.

You see their maize? They're two months ahead of us.

Finally the coach crossed the motor causeway to the Queen of Cities. In the vaporetto the men stood up very straight, as if on parade. This was because they were reminded of the first time they had left the village as conscripts in the army. The women lounged on the deck seats, and the younger ones pulled up their skirts to bare their legs to the sun. The vaporetto swayed first to one side and then to the other, like a woman pedaling very slowly on a bicycle.

How would you like a white suit like the ship's captain?

Look at those insects!

Where?

There!

She's been drinking!

He must change it every day.

Look! Along the water line.

Good God, yes, thousands of them.

They come up for the sun.

They're crabs.

I've never seen crabs that size.

You don't know what to look at.

I tell you, it looks like a flood.

You couldn't make cheese here!

They disembarked at the Piazza San Marco and climbed the circular staircase of the Campanile. Afterwards the men were thirsty and insisted upon having a drink in one of the cafés on the piazza, which Napoleon called the largest ballroom in Europe.

It costs more to piss here than to drink a whole case at home!

Inside the café he noticed a poster announcing a festival organised by *L'Unità*, the Communist daily newspaper. Why not?

They crossed the Bridge of Sighs and stopped beneath a statue of Eve in the courtyard of the Doge's Palace.

It's a wife like that you need!

Later the men climbed onto the terrace of the Cathedral of San Marco to look at the horses.

The festival was to be held on the island of Giudecca. From the Doge's Palace he could see the coloured lights decorating the buildings across the water and from time to time he heard a strain of music.

If you're not at the bus station by two, we'll know they drowned you.

He's more adventurous than the rest of you men!

He sat in the stern of the vaporetto with his instrument case on his knees.

You're not from here.

These words were addressed to him by a young woman with magenta lipstick and white sandals.

How is that?

You look too quiet.

You know what I have in this box?

She shook her head. She had glasses and her black hair was drawn back in a chignon.

A trombone.

It's not true, she cried. Play it! Please, play something.

Not here on the boat, he said. Are you going to the festival?

If you brought it with you, you must have had the idea of playing it.

We came from the mountains. I didn't want to leave it in the bus.

Around her neck was a white necklace.

You, do you live down here?

In Mestri, across the bay, where the oil tanks are. And you —I'd say you work on a farm.

How do you know?

I can smell the cows.

If she had been a man, he would have hit her.

What do you think I smell of?

Scent.

Correct. I work in a chemist's shop.

One look at your hands told me you didn't work with them.

Do you know what my father calls that?

No.

Infantile proletarianism.

He said nothing. Perhaps it was a Venetian expression.

The vaporetto was approaching the island. Hung from the first-storey windows on the far side of the piazza were bande-rolas with slogans printed on them. He could make out the hammer and sickle. As he stepped ashore, he held his instrument case tightly under his arm. The festival, he reminded himself, was organised by the Communist Party, but this did not mean there were no thieves there. He could spot them already.

Do you like dancing? she asked.

I can't dance carrying this.

Give it to me.

She disappeared with his instrument case into one of the nearby buildings.

And if it's stolen? he said, when she came back empty-handed.

Comrade, she replied, this is a workers' festival, and workers do not steal from one another.

Peasants do! he said.

What is your name?

Bruno. And yours?

Marietta.

He held up his arm for her to take his hand. He did not dance like a man from here, she thought. He was more single-minded, as if, when dancing, he put everything else out of his mind.

What is it like on your mountain?

There are rhodos and wild goats.

Rhodos?

Little bushes of flowers.

Pink?

Blood-red.

How do they vote in your village?

For the right.

And you?

I vote for anyone who promises to raise the price of milk.

That isn't good for the workers.

Milk is all we have to sell.

They were dancing round a plane tree in a corner of the piazza. In the tree was a loudspeaker, perched like an owl on one of the branches.

You came here alone? she asked.

With the whole band.

A band of friends?

The brass band of the village.

The next time the owl fell silent he proposed that they should have a drink. She guided him to a table beneath a gigantic portrait, drawn on a sheet and hung from the top windows of a house. The painted face was so large that even the flanks of the nose had been drawn with a six-inch house-painter's brush. They looked up at it together.

Do you live alone? she asked.

Yes, I've lived alone for eight years. A fifth of my life.

She liked the way he hesitated before speaking, it was very deliberate, as if each time he answered one of her questions, he came to the door of a house, opened it to a visitor, and then spoke.

How many mirrors do you have at home? She asked this as if it were a schoolgirl's riddle.

He paused to count.

One over the sink, one over the drinking trough outside.

She laughed. He poured out more white wine.

That's Karl Marx, isn't it? He nodded up at the sheet.

Marx was a great prophet. What do you see in the future? she asked.

The rich getting richer.

I mean your future.

Mine? Everything depends upon my health.

You don't look sick to me.

If you're sent to hospital when you are sick, your dog doesn't look after your cows. I live alone.

She raised her glass to his. I think I could find you work in Mestri.

He was looking at her small feet, thinking: everything between a man and a woman is a question of how much you give up of one thing to have another—an exchange.

You are bound to be influenced by the property relations of which you are a part. Her voice was tender, as if she were explaining something intimate. The Kulaks sided with the bourgeoisie, and the little peasants with the petit bourgeoisie. You are wrong to think only about the price of milk.

She comes, he told himself, from this place of water and islands where there is no earth at all.

The fact is peasants will disappear, she continued, the future lies elsewhere.

I'd like to have children, he said.

You have to find a wife.

He poured out more wine.

You'd find a wife if you moved here.

I'd cut off my right hand rather than work in a factory.

All the men dancing there, she said, they're nearly all factory workers.

He had never seen so many men in white shirts. They wore their shirts tied round their waists to show off their stomachs. They were as cunning as weasels. Their cuffs were rolled back only halfway up their forearms, as if they had just got out of bed.

Do they caress well? he asked.

Who?

The weasels over there.

Caress?

What a man should do to a woman.

Let's dance, she said.

The owl was hooting a tango.

Who's milking the cows tonight? she whispered.

Who am I dancing with?

Marietta is dancing with Bruno, she said, as he pulled her hand up and looked along their arms—as if taking aim with a gun.

As the tempo increased they advanced and turned more and more quickly. People began to watch them. His shirt and his heavy shoes announced he was from the country. But he danced well, they made a couple. Some of the bystanders began to clap in time with the music. It was like watching a duel—a duel between the paving stones and their four feet. How long would they keep it up?

Now they were walking down a narrow street, with old men on wicker chairs, and grandmothers playing with balloons to amuse their grandchildren. At the end of the street was suspended another gigantic portrait: a great domed head, like a beehive of thought, wearing glasses.

That's Gramsci.

He put his arm round her shoulders so that she could lean her head against his damp flannel shirt.

Antonio Gramsci, she said. He taught us all.

You wouldn't mistake him for a horse dealer! he said.

Past the portrait, they came to a cobbled quayside overlooking the lagoon toward Murano. In places grass had grown over the cobbles. He stared across the black water and she, carrying her sandals, wandered over to an abandoned gondola, moored by the corner of the Rio di Santa Eufemia. She sat down on the platform by the stern near the wooden oarlock. Sun and water had stripped the gondola of its paint, which was now wood grey. It must once have belonged to a wine merchant, for several demijohns lay on their sides in the prow.

Do you think they are empty? she asked him.

Instead of answering, he jumped into the gondola, which rocked violently. Making his way forward to the prow, he did his best to correct every lurch by leaning in the opposite direction, like someone dancing in a conga line.

Sit down, for God's sake, sit down! she shouted.

She was crouching in the bottom of the boat. Its sides were smacking the water and splashing the air.

He picked up a demijohn and held it against the sky with one hand as if wringing the neck of a goose.

Empty! he boomed.

Sit! she shrieked. Sit!

This is how they found themselves lying on the rush mat in the bottom of the gondola. After a while the smacking of the water ceased and a quiet lapping took its place. Yet the calm did not last long. Soon the gondola was again lurching from side to side with water dripping from its gunwales and its staves thumping the lagoon.

If we capsize, can you swim? she whispered.

No.

Yes, Bruno, yes, yes, yes . . .

Afterwards they lay on their backs, panting.

Look at the stars. Don't they make you feel small? she said.

The stars look down at us, she continued, and sometimes I think everything, everything except killing, everything takes so long because they are so far away.

His other hand was trailing in the water. Her teeth bit his ear.

The world changes so slowly.

His hand from the water grasped her breast.

One day there'll be no more classes. I believe that, don't you? she murmured and pulled his head down to her other breast.

There's always been good and bad, he said.

We're making progress, don't you believe that?

All our ancestors asked the same thing, he said, you and I will never know in this life why it was made the way it is.

He entered her again. The gondola smacked the water and splashed the air.

When they crossed the narrow island to the pierhead, where the last vaporetto would stop, the music was over. Only a few drunks, immobile as statues, remained in the piazza. Marietta went to fetch his instrument case. He gazed across the lagoon. He could see the bell-tower they had climbed. The guide said it had toppled over at the beginning of the century. No roots. He remembered the date: 14th July 1902, the year of his father's birth. To the right there were still lights in the Doge's Palace. According to the guide, the palace had been destroyed or partly destroyed by fire seven times. There had never been peace in that building. Too much power and no roots. One day it would be robbed and pillaged and after that it would be used as a hen house.

Marietta handed him his instrument case.

Play for me. Play me something.

He put the case down on the quayside. Out of his pocket he took a small mouth organ, and turning toward the Doge's Palace, began to play. The music was speaking to him.

Before it is light—

She was staring at his back, relaxed and downcast like the back of a man peeing, except that his hands were to his mouth.

—Before it is light . . . when you've dressed and gone into the stable—

With her fingers she was touching the nape of his neck.

—the animals are lying there—

She was pressing her hand between his shoulder blades and could feel his lungs and the music in the roof of his mouth.

—lying there on beech leaves, and your tiredness like a child you have dragged from its sleep—

Her hand felt under the belt of his trousers.

—and through the window you see the span of the stars—

She noticed that one of his bootlaces was undone. She knelt down to tie it for him.

—the span of the stars into whose well we are thrown at birth like salt into water—

Neither of them noticed the vaporetto approaching the pierhead.

Come to Mestri, she sighed, come to Mestri. I'll find you work.

The bus left at 3 A.M. Most of the band wanted to sleep. Some husbands put their heads on their wives' shoulders, in other cases the wife leaned her head against her man. The lights were switched out one by one as the coach took the road for Verona. The young drummer sitting beside Bruno tried one last joke.

Do you know what hell is?

Do you?

Hell is where bottles have two holes and women have none.

[For Jacob]

Hell begins with hope. If we didn't have any hopes we wouldn't suffer. We'd be like ... rocks against the sky. (p171)
... It's only in hell, my love, that we find each other. (p180)

Keep tears
My heart
For prose.

Train
Flammes bleues
Fleurs jaunes.
In the ditches
I am water.
Between
Grow kingcups of your childhood.
Sunk in my eyes
Skies of the churchyard.
Through arteries
Of gravel
Whispering to my grasses
The blood of good-byes.
Flammes bleues
Fleurs jaunes
Their railways.

1985/86

John Berger, born in London in 1926, is well known as a
novelist, screenwriter, documentary writer, and art critic.
His books include *The Sense of Sight, About Looking,
The Success and Failure of Picasso, Ways of Seeing,
Art and Revolution,* and the award-winning novel *G,*
among many others.

He now lives and works in a small French peasant
community. This milieu is the setting for *Pig Earth*
and *Once in Europa,* the first two volumes of a trilogy
that tells, in fictional form, of the peasant's odyssey
from village to metropolis.